Praise for **Self Care**

"Leigh Stein's latest novel is as decadent and brutal as a vampire facial. It's an exposé of feel-good feminism, an indictment of contemporary capitalism, and an absolute treat to read. This book will make you laugh, gasp, and vow to get off social media for good—and it'll understand when you can't help but log right back on."

—Julia Phillips, author of National Book Award finalist *Disappearing Earth*

"*Self Care* is a skewering mockumentary about influencer culture, internet feminism, and the infinite ways that big tech capitalizes on our worst fears and insecurities. Utterly teeming with humor, this is exactly the sort of book that Dorothy Parker would have written if she'd been reincarnated as an Instagram celebrity."

—Catherine Lacey, author of *The Answers* and *Certain American States*

"Wickedly talented Leigh Stein—for my money, one of our sharpest millennial writers—knows the internet, and she's used that intimate knowledge to write a pitch-perfect novel for our times. *Self Care* is a hilarious and sneakily moving send-up of what it means to try and live when every move you make is observed and dissected online, by a writer who sees the truth and says it with so much humor and heart you'll laugh (and maybe cry) out loud."

—Julie Buntin, author of *Marlena*

"A titillating satire about our quest for validation and the lengths that some will go to for #selfactualization, *Self Care* is an intelligent, delightful read that will make your mind (and epidermis!) glow."

—Courtney Maum, author of *Touch* and *Costalegre*

"I couldn't stop laughing. I loved it."

—Edan Lepucki, author of *Woman No. 17*

Praise for **The Fallback Plan**

"Beautiful, funny, thrilling, and true."   —Gary Shteyngart

"Highbrow brilliant."   —*New York*

"*The Fallback Plan* is to this generation what Rick Moody's *The Ice Storm* was to a previous generation, and *The Catcher in the Rye* before that."   —*Los Angeles Review of Books*

PENGUIN BOOKS

Self Care

Leigh Stein is the author of the acclaimed 2012 novel *The Fallback Plan*, a poetry collection published the same year, and the 2016 memoir, *Land of Enchantment*. From 2014 to 2017, she ran a secret Facebook group of forty thousand women writers, in her role as cofounder and executive director of Out of the Binders/BinderCon, a feminist nonprofit organization. She's been called a "leading feminist" by *The Washington Post* and "poet laureate of *The Bachelor*" by *The Cut*.

Self Care

A Novel

Leigh Stein

PENGUIN BOOKS

PENGUIN BOOKS
An imprint of Penguin Random House LLC
penguinrandomhouse.com

LIBRARY OF CONGRESS CATALOGING-IN-PUBLICATION DATA
Names: Stein, Leigh, 1984– author.
Title: Self care : a novel / Leigh Stein.
Description: New York City : Penguin Books, [2020]
Identifiers: LCCN 2019049527 (print) | LCCN 2019049528 (ebook) |
ISBN 9780143135197 (paperback) | ISBN 9780525506867 (ebook)
Classification: LCC PS3619.T465 S45 2020 (print) |
LCC PS3619.T465 (ebook) | DDC 813/.6–dc23
LC record available at https://lccn.loc.gov/2019049527
LC ebook record available at https://lccn.loc.gov/2019049528

Printed in the United States of America
3 5 7 9 10 8 6 4 2

Set in Sabon Next LT Pro
Designed by Alexis Farabaugh

Woman lives her body as seen by another.

—Sandra Lee Bartky

If you think the internet is terrible now, just wait a while.

—Balk's Third Law

Self
Care

When's the Last Time You Put Yourself First?

Maren

By the time Devin found me, I'd been at the office for fourteen hours and was lying on a lavender velvet chaise, fortifying myself with room-temperature-staff-kitchen chardonnay that I'd poured into a "MALE TEARS" mug, scrolling through my various feeds, using multiple search terms, absorbing every abusive thing people were saying about me, @MarenGelb, M**en G**b, *libtard*, *feminazi*, *stupid fucking cunt*.

I wasn't crying. I felt pleasantly numb. With an insatiable hunger for knowing, I kept compulsively refreshing, in search of the worst. The infinite scroll prevented me from ever hitting bottom.

The elevator ding signaled her arrival. "Babe?"

I raised my mug in the air.

"You're here! People are worried about you. Your phone is off."

"I turned it on Do Not Disturb so I could OD on the internet in peace."

Devin tossed her coat over an ergonomic exercise ball chair.

Her blond hair was still damp from showering after her exercise class, so I knew she wasn't *too* concerned about me, not so concerned that she'd miss an opportunity to burn six hundred calories. She was wearing her "Namaslay" T-shirt.

After a bottle of wine, I'd ditched my sweater and was down to my BreastNest, a garment I'd ordered online. It's a spongy beige sack you can wear for support if even the idea of clasping a bra is *too much*.

"Sit next to me," I said. "You smell good."

"What are you drinking?"

"Kombucha," I said.

I'd been working late, revising the competitive advantage slide for our pitch deck. Everyone else had gone home. The song of my inbox played at a slower tempo after dark—it was the only time of day I could get anything done. I took a break to check Twitter, and without asking anyone's permission or doing a SWOT analysis, I made a joke. Or I thought it was a joke. Definitely an anger-based joke, I can admit that now. It seemed more obviously funny at the time.

"What if you just deleted the tweet?" she said.

"Too late. They already showed it on Anderson Cooper."

I played the clip for her on my phone. *Leading feminist Maren Gelb is causing waves tonight with what some on the right are calling a dog whistle to other activists about the president's daughter and her*—I had to turn it off. I couldn't watch it again.

"Don't worry," Devin said. "No one watches Anderson Cooper."

"I watch Anderson Cooper."

"Well, you're my elder." Devin smiled and the highlighter

around her eyes shimmered with optimism. "Give me the phone, Maren."

"Why, what are you going to do with it?"

"I'm just going to babysit it while you clean up."

"Wait," I snapped. My left hand was a claw that had evolved to grip this little screen until I died. "Can I show you just one?" We both knew I was stalling. "Look at this douche in Palo Alto with half a million followers, saying, '@MarenGelb is an example of the leadership principal when they go low, we go lower. Did I get that right? Hashtag AllLivesMatter.' He doesn't even know how to spell *principle*! 'All Lives Matter'? Seriously? Do you see this?"

Devin put my phone in her back pocket without even looking at the screen. I needed another drink.

"Well," I said, "the good news is I figured out what our competitive advantage is."

"Let me guess. Our badass cofounders?" She pointed at me and made her hands into a heart.

"No."

"Wait, don't tell me. Our seamless integration of sponsored content and organically sourced influencers?"

"No," I said. "The worse it gets—I mean the more women who are outraged and terrified and suffering—the more our user base grows. The more the network scales."

It was happening right now. A hundred new members a minute. The more I was attacked by right-wing trolls, the more women on the left rallied to support me. I was smart enough to retweet all the rape threats (mostly in the "too ugly to rape" genre) I was getting and ask women to create accounts at Richual, the social network Devin and I had built as a world without men—where women could actually take care of themselves.

Richual asked: when's the last time you put yourself first? Our app pressed a pause button on all the bullshit in daily life. You could track your meditation minutes and ounces of water consumed and REM sleep and macros and upcoming Mercury retrogrades and see who among your friends was best at prioritizing #metime, based on how many hours a day they spent on the app. It was a virtual space where @SmokyMountainHeartOpener posted videos of herself doing forearm stands in a thong leotard and @PussyGrabsBack shared photos of her feet soaking in Epsom salt after a march.

It was the digital sanctuary where you went to unload your pain.

We earned revenue from the brands who offered solutions to that pain: serums and creams, juices and dusts, clays and scrubs, drugs and masks, oils and enemas, scraping and purging, vaping and waxing, lifting and lengthening, straightening and defining, detox and retox, the cycle of life.

Devin was the face of Richual. She was also the body. She was literally the "after" photo in a piece of branded content promoting a thirty-day cleanse. T-shirt slogans popped on her flat chest. Her collarbone was usually exposed and opalescent. She was small enough that she appeared appropriately human-size in photographs taken at red carpet launches, while I stood to one side like her zaftig cousin visiting from another country—the country of Wisconsin.

Devin hid the work it took to make that body. I wore my work like a second, visible skin. Over the course of eighteen months, I'd gone from a size 8 to a 14 and upped my Zoloft prescription twice. My thighs rubbed together when I walked in a dress. The internet told me this was normal. The internet showed me ads for nontoxic anti-chafing gel.

No one ever called us by the other's name.

Devin went to the beauty closet and came back with a tube of Missha Super Aqua Cell Renew Snail Sleeping Mask with 15 percent snail slime extract "from healthy snails born within five to six months" for "strengthening the skin barrier in a natural way."

"Try this and we'll take a selfie and I'll post it to my account so everyone knows you're okay," Devin said. She picked my wrinkled sweater off the floor and I held my arms up like a toddler, so she could dress me.

"The tweet is gonna be good for us, you'll see," I said. "Don't worry about the tweet."

FOR IMMEDIATE RELEASE

February 24, 2017

RICHUAL CEO DEVIN AVERY
WISHES COO MAREN GELB "GOOD
VIBES" FOR HER RECOVERY

Maren Gelb deeply regrets the violent language she
posted on Twitter yesterday in regards to a family
member of POTUS. Her tweet does not in any way
reflect the values of Richual, the most inclusive
community platform for women to cultivate the
practice of self-care and change the world by changing ourselves. CEO Devin Avery assures the Richual
community that Maren's joke was meant to be
perceived as "dark humor," like "Melissa McCarthy,"
and not as a threat to the health or safety of the
first daughter.

"Maren is the most selfless, empathic person I know,"
Avery says. "I could not have done this without her
as my work wife, and I'm sending so many good
vibes her way."

In the words of one of our faves, Audre Lorde,
"Caring for myself is not self-indulgence, it is self-
preservation. And that is an act of political warfare,"
but "warfare" is up to each person to decide for

herself, and at Richual, we believe that all people are
human beings. We trust the community will join us
in support of Maren, while she realigns her spirit and
health with our core values of respite, recalibration,
and resilience. #Namaste

About Us: *Richual is a pioneer in the wellness space, using social technology to connect, cure, and catalyze women to be global change-makers through the simple act of self-care.*

Devin

Women are people.
All people are human beings.
Believe women.
Do better.
Self-care is not selfish.
Don't read the comments.
You are more than a digital footprint.
The political is personal.
Stay woke.
Calm the fuck down.

With a single tweet, Maren had broken at least two of Richual's Ten Commandments stenciled in fuchsia and sherbet on the wall by reception. How could she say she believed women when she didn't believe that having a woman who could advocate for better family leave policies to her dad was a good thing for women? A girl I knew in college was now doing marketing for a startup using nanotechnology to build air filters that eradicate mold toxicity on the molecular level and the guy who had the job before *her* had a younger brother (adopted) who once dated Tiffany and that was how I was able to get a meeting with someone on Ivanka's team about inviting her to join our exclusive sorority of Richual influencers, after it came to me in a dream one night, the kind of high-quality native content related to juggling entrepreneurship, motherhood, politics, and gardening she could put out there as @Fir$tDaughter, but Maren flushed that potential partnership down the toilet.

When I asked her to at least explain the tweet to me, why she thought it was funny, she just sent me a link to an article about "punching up" in comedy and said, "Educate yourself."

I wasn't mad, not after I did my rounds of kapalabhati this morning, but I was concerned. Maren practiced the least amount of self-care of anyone I knew. Imagine if the COO of Sweetgreen ate McDonald's for lunch every day. You'd be like, *Wut*?

I'd seen Maren like this before. When I met her at a retreat for solopreneurs in New Orleans, she was in a very dark place. You could tell she was one of the scholarship recipients by how I found her during the continental breakfast wrapping mini muffins in paper napkins to save in her purse for lunch. Now that I think of it, it wasn't really a purse so much as it was a "Free Pussy Riot" tote bag. "I want to mentor *that* one," I told the organizers. She was working for a charity and had come to the retreat to learn entrepreneurship so she could get better at fundraising. I wanted to do a full makeover, starting with the food types that suited her dosha, but when she showed me the charity website, we had to start there.

"Honestly? You need to invest in a redesign," I told her. "You only have one chance to make a first impression on me and this is not mobile-friendly. I can't share this link with my friends and ask them to donate if it's not cute, you know?"

Maren put her head in her hands. I could tell I was breaking through to her by the way she was breaking down. "You want to make money, don't you?" I asked. She nodded her head without looking at me. "Like, a *lot* of money, right?" Another nod.

Overnight, she redesigned the website herself, so that it was more *pink* overall and the Donate Now button stood out in mint green, the color of money, not in an aggressive way but in a way that made you feel generous, like you were building Barbie's Dreamhouse for women who were less fortunate than you.

No matter what I suggested Maren do—including actually ask herself if she wanted to be leading a nonprofit where everyone took her for granted—she did it. We roleplayed different scenarios where she would find herself one-on-one with a woman with a high net worth. I told her the secret to asking for money was to never actually mention money at all.

"Pretend I'm seventy-eight, I'm a widow, my name is Frances but all my friends call me Fifi, and I have a bichon frise on my lap.

"Pretend I'm the young heiress to an alcoholic beverage distributor fortune and I grew up in a household that values philanthropy and you happen to run into me at SoulCycle in East Hampton.

"Pretend my family built their wealth doing something very bad for the environment or something and I feel very, very guilty, and you can help me feel better."

Finally, I said, "Before she died, my mom started a small foundation that gives art grants in New York City. I know she would have been interested in the work you're doing and I'd like to donate five thousand dollars."

"Is this part of the roleplay?"

"No! I'm being serious."

Maren's nose turned bright red and then she started to cry. I'd never seen someone so genuinely grateful about so little money. It was super satisfying, like when you're trying to get the last glob of jelly cleanser from a tube and you're shaking and shaking it upside down and it squirts out all at once. I wondered what it would be like to collaborate on something, if I could find us some funding. Maren could resign from her pointless job and we could do work that actually made a difference—at scale.

The only story sexier than a woman under thirty starting a company was *two* women under thirty starting a company. Cover story in *Fast Company*, profile in the Styles section, slideshow on Vogue dot com: "Workplace as Vulva—And Why Not?" Our interior designer conceptualized our layout and decor to be a visual representation of our brand: female-facing, luxurious yet accessible, and totally transparent. Break boundaries by literally having none. My office was one of the few with walls and a door, but they were glass walls, and the door itself was just a glass wall with a handle.

From my desk, I could see the entire floor of my small but

dedicated kingdom, a dozen ladies wearing noise-canceling head-phones, sitting at long marbled-pink tables, or ruining their tho-racic spines on jewel-toned velvet couches. Emerald and sapphire, garnet and citrine. Even the girl we hired to be the receptionist was usually wearing headphones, which someone should really do something about.

Last night, I told Maren she needed to take some PTO and the office definitely felt more chill without her. Probably because nothing was on fire. I put some lavender essential oil in the stone diffuser on my desk and took a deep breath. In between a lilac Pusheenicorn I got from Secret Santa and a vase of pink ranuncu-lus, I had a little inspiration library: *The Glitter Plan*, *Big Magic*, *Sparkle*, *You Are a Badass*, *You Yes You Are a Unicorn*, *Style Your Mind*, *Mind Your Magic*, *The Subtle Art of Not Giving a F*ck*, *Peace Is Every Breath: A Practice for Our Busy Lives*.

Thich Nhat Hanh says, "When another person makes you suf-fer, it is because he suffers deeply within himself," and I knew that Maren must be suffering deeply. She definitely didn't seem as grateful as she used to be. I slipped on my therapeutic gel toe separators, curled up in the papasan chair in the corner of my of-fice, and googled *burnout or depression which more dangerous* and *leaky gut SSRI addiction* and *pitta-deranged panchakarma* and *act-ing out behavior alkaline reset hormone imbalance clean recipe juice fast greens tonic*.

"Is now a good time?" Khadijah was knocking on the glass wall to my office.

I waved her in. "Did you see the press release?"

"Uh-huh."

"I thought it was pretty good, right?"

"Do you want to start with the editorial calendar for the rest of Black History Month or do you want to see the slideshow of your morning routine?"

"Slideshow! Here, you sit at my desk," I said. I pulled my chair closer so I could see her laptop. Khadijah was SVP of editorial strategy and she'd earned every letter in that title because she did the job of, like, ten people: writing the copy, editing the copy, taking the photos, editing the photos, A/B testing the headlines, publishing eight posts a day. She was almost better at writing in my voice than I was.

> Ladies, I have a confession to make. When I was in college a hundred years ago, my morning routine used to go something like this: I would hit "snooze" two or three times before jumping in the shower, put my wet hair in a bun because I didn't have the time to blow-dry, and grab a bacon, egg, and cheese from a food cart on my way to class. My chin kept breaking out and my legs were covered in patches of scaly eczema. I always felt like if I could just find an extra thirty minutes somewhere, I could catch up, but I never found it.
>
> Now I know that anyone who wants to actually get anything done today needs to get up before dawn, so let's get dark with this dinacharya.

"Damn, girl," I said. "That sounds just like me." We knew from Maren's analytics that posts that started with "I have a confession to make" or "I have a secret to admit" or "There's something I've never told anyone before" got the most traffic and elicited the most emotional responses in the comments section. "But I wonder if the eczema bit is TMI?" I was so in tune with my body that even *thinking* about eczema made me want to itch until I bled.

She deleted it.

"And we're going to define *dinacharya* somewhere?"

"In a sidebar," she said.

I watched over her shoulder as she flipped through the slideshow. There I was, smiling at my own reflection in my bathroom mirror, holding up my silver tongue scraper (not my *actual* scraper but a new one for the shoot); me in a white crop top doing ardha chandra chapasana as the sun rose above the East River, light dappling my yoga mat. In the next slide, I'm watching the sunrise out the window, holding an earthen Kintsukuroi bowl of overnight oats and chia seeds with coconut sugar.

"Is there anything we can do about my jaw?" I tapped her screen with the tip of my nail. I hated how my underbite looked in photographs. Having spent the entirety of my twenties sharing my life on social media, I was very aware of my angles, conscious of the face I allowed the world to see.

In Photoshop, Khadijah fixed my face one pixel at a time. When we first launched, Maren had explained to me, *If we're going to be two white girls with a startup, we can't be two white girls who don't know we're white. I don't want any press that's like, "They didn't get the diversity memo."* I agreed that I was white, but I didn't feel as bad about it as Maren did. Khadijah was our very first hire. In the media kit photos, her box braids looked bananas. Maren wanted to give her 5 percent equity because of reparations, but I talked her down to 2.5.

I still was confused about whether I was supposed to let Khadijah know that I knew she was black or if I was supposed to pretend that her blackness never crossed my mind.

"Your skin looks great," I said. "Are you using hyaluronic acid?"

"Nope."

"Pore-refining mask?"

"I'm not doing anything different," she said, trying to suppress a yawn. For the shoot, she'd had to arrive at my apartment before dawn.

"Maybe it's just that color on you," I said. "What is it, MAC Rebel?"

"Thanks," she said. "I'll get this posted as soon as I finish editing your face."

"Don't stay too late tonight, okay?"

She'd already put her headphones back on so I wasn't sure if she heard me.

I should wear more lipstick, I thought, looking at myself in selfie mode on my phone. But my lips were thin, and drawing attention to them would draw attention to my jaw, which was more Samantha Bee than Reese Witherspoon. Not that I didn't totally admire them both for being older women who were still visible in public.

There is a typo in a headline on the site , Maren texted with a screenshot.

You are supposed to be resting!!!!!

I am resting. I am in bed right now.

You are working.

Not working, just scrolling.

She couldn't turn it off, not even for a day.

Hey, I texted Evan. He was our first investor, the person who'd made all this possible. I tried to only ask him for favors when it was truly necessary.

Sup

Can we use your house this weekend? I think Maren needs detox.

Am I invited?

Ummmmmmm, I said. I knew what he was really asking, but my hands were full with Maren. Girls' trip?

Totes magotes, he said. Just lmk when you're coming by for the keys.

Maren

"As soon as I saw the tweet, I knew I wanted to help," Evan said. "Are you okay?"

"I'm okay. I mean I will be."

"Because I'm sorry to tell you this, but you look like shit," he said and we both laughed. I had to laugh. In a couple of weeks, Evan and I would be in back-to-back meetings with VCs. "Sleep-deprived teen goth who swears these jeans must have shrunk in the wash" was not the best look for me to deliver our value prop. Male founders could get away with a sloppy genius aesthetic, but I had to be a brand ambassador for self-care.

"So take the weekend—take the whole week if you need it. My parents hardly ever go up to the house anymore. Put your phone on airplane mode, light a fire, take a bath, whatever you need to get back in fighting shape. And most importantly?"

"Yes?"

"Don't read the comments."

"Too late," Devin and I said at the same time.

Evan's penthouse on Rivington was all high ceilings and right angles and cold daylight. The open kitchen had a distressed reclaimed wood light fixture with vintage Edison bulbs hanging from it, the exposed filaments like fairies trapped upside down in jars. Floor-to-ceiling windows overlooked a wraparound terrace and views of Lower Manhattan. Evan had made a small fortune while he was still at Wharton, when the mobile-friendly cryptocurrency trading bot he built was acquired by one of the world's largest banks. But more people knew him as the *Bachelorette* runner-up who abandoned the bachelorette during the rose ceremony of the fantasy suite episode in a radical protest of the show's amplification of toxic masculinity. "I will no longer be complicit," he said, before ripping off his mic and riding off into the tropical night, shirtless, on a motorcycle. Girls at home, gripping their third goblets of rosé, lost their minds, googled *toxic masculinity*, started petitions for Evan to become the next bachelor, even as he told TMZ he was done with the franchise.

He was our first investor and one of our most trusted advisors, the guru behind our exit strategy. Through his connections, he'd helped us raise five million in our series A.

"Alexa!" Evan yelled in the direction of the living room. "Play the Julie Ruin."

"Shuffling songs by the Julie Ruin on Amazon Music," a pleasant woman's voice answered and a bouncy keyboard intro sounded through the speaker.

It was only polite to stay beyond the length of a single song, let

Evan show us how he synced all his home furnishings to voice-activated electronic devices.

"Siri. What. Do. I. Have. In. The. Fridge," he said, and photographs of a milk carton, a hunk of cheese, and a six-pack of Stella scrolled across the screen of his iPhone. "This has integrated functionality with synchronous voice activation and live feed from the interior cameras. I get notifications when I'm out of beer. My boy Jay? He's at Samsung now. I get beta versions of everything."

"Is it just me or is the future men yelling at computers named after women? And the woman always answering with a smile in her voice?" I said.

"Who's yelling?"

"You're commanding," Devin suggested.

"I'm sure there's a setting to change the gender of the AI."

I didn't think he was right, but I also had to be careful about how many times a day I told other people they were wrong. I had to give Evan credit—he was one of the first people to really get what Devin and I were trying to do. A couple of years before, we were naive and arrogant enough to think that our idea would be a no-brainer for female angel investors, but we got no after no after no. Their wellness portfolio was full, or they didn't see the need for yet another social media platform they would have to check and monitor (no, it's a *community*, we insisted), or we couldn't convince them that self-care was a concept that could be packaged, marketed, sold. We lost one pitch competition to an app that would tell you how long the line was for each women's restroom at a venue like Madison Square Garden; their "revenue model" was to run ads for antiperspirant and low-cal Moscato.

The founders were two energetic white guys wearing short-sleeved shirts buttoned up to their necks and Clark Kent glasses. *If you really want to disrupt women's restrooms*, I thought, *just add more fucking stalls.*

Along the upstairs hallway Evan had a series of framed movie posters: *Kill Bill, Mad Max: Fury Road, Silence of the Lambs, Thelma and Louise, Erin Brockovich.* I could almost hear the ghostly cries of all the girls Evan led down this hall: *OMG, I love that movie.*

"Bedroom TV up!" he yelled and I watched from the doorway to the master as a flatscreen rose slowly from the bench at the foot of the bed.

Devin raised her eyebrows at me, trying to encourage more enthusiasm on my end. *Don't you want to be rich, rich like this?* This was an aspirational field trip, to show us what was possible, if we kept up the grind.

My fantasies were almost too boring to put on a vision board: Pay off $68,000 of student loan debt from NYU. Get my mom a new car to replace her 2002 Saturn. Buy an item from Duane Reade that cost more than twenty dollars without first checking my bank account balance.

Richual was making money, but we were putting it all back into the company. "You have to spend money to make money!" Evan liked to remind us; he was always getting on my case for trying to cut costs in any way. "This isn't a 501(c)(3), Maren. You're in the weeds again."

But I liked being in the weeds. There was no vertigo down in the swamp, no sense of falling off a high cliff of unrealistic projections or expectations. Running a function on a column of cells was my style of self-soothing. If I could isolate the point at which our social spend stopped effectively acquiring users, didn't they want to know? And were we worrying enough about providing value to our current users? Even when I wasn't staring at a timeline of key performance indicators on my laptop screen, numbers and words scrolled through my brain like a Jenny Holzer installation of my own self-loathing: "BEING A GOOD GIRL IS WORTH NO MORE THAN $50,000 SO ADJUST YOUR EXPECTATIONS OR BEHAVIOR." That's what Devin and I were each making—a childless millennial living wage in any city but New York—but I had a pile of credit card debt ($4,000 dental implant; $1,000 for new clothes, produced at ethical garment factories that comply with all labor laws, to upgrade my ill-fitting thrift store "here's a woman who is so body positive she doesn't own a mirror" wardrobe; $1,200 for a weekend in Miami because what's another $1,200 when you're already $5,000 in the hole?) on top of my student loans.

Meanwhile, Devin had a multimillion-dollar safety net—her inheritance and the life insurance from her dad's sudden death, plus the money from the sale of the apartment she'd grown up in. I waffled between resentment (*Couldn't she see how much of a difference an extra ten grand would make in my life? Why did it have to be fifty-fifty?*) and pity (*Both her parents died when she was only in her twenties*).

For Christmas, she'd given me a one-month subscription ($650) to Euphebe, a plant-based meal-delivery service, which seemed like an expensive way of telling me she'd noticed the weight I'd gained since we launched.

I made her a hooped cross-stitch of a bar graph showing our user growth over the past six months. While she'd been restricting, I'd been producing.

There was a peal of laughter. Devin had her back up against the door to the walk-in closet, playfully pushing Evan away. Evan didn't always have the best instincts in terms of personal space. He was a close-talker, someone who made you feel like he was giving you all of his attention, whether you wanted it or not. Our younger staff lost their shit when he came by the office. Maybe it was his status as a minor TV personality, or maybe it was just the rarity of having a man around HQ. I once heard our receptionist describe Evan's scruffily bearded and vaguely irresponsible attractiveness quotient as "retro Mark Ruffalo."

We needed to get out of here.

"Thanks, Evan," I said. "For everything. Your place is great. I love it." My depression gave me the personality of a fembot, spewing phrases I'd been programmed with. But Evan didn't seem to notice.

He pulled out a ring of at least twenty keys. "You won't need all these," he said, "but the yellow one's the front door, the red one is the doorknob, this one is for the barn slash pool house, and I think these are for the guest suite above the garage. There are other outbuildings but those don't matter. Mailbox key you won't need."

"Thanks, Evan. Seriously."

"Come here," he said, drawing me in for a side hug. Up close, I noticed a poppy seed in his teeth and the blackheads at the tip of his nose. "Get some rest, and then we're back in the clouds, right? Ten thousand feet?" He held up a hand for a high five.

• • •

In the elevator, I said, "Hey, girl, I've been known to raise some capital, but I couldn't figure out how to raise my TV until I met you."

"Siri, what beverage. Can I offer. To this female," Devin said into her phone.

I appreciated the emotional labor she put into making fun of Evan for me. Devin was at Barnard at the same time his younger brother was at Columbia and they were like family—a weirdly incestuous family. According to Evan, Devin was one of the few women he could be "real" with, because others saw him as a well-connected ATM. (I saw him as a well-connected ATM.)

Outside, John was waiting for us in the rental car. Devin was in charge of the playlist, and I sat in the backseat and held a gallon tub of rice and mung beans that she promised would "de-age" me. She couldn't resist a before and after. John had never been Devin's number-one fan, but I convinced him that he needed a relaxing weekend in the country, too.

First up: "Shape of You" by Ed Sheeran and Devin started to dance in the passenger seat, swimming backward with her fists, while John cursed under his breath, trying to get on the FDR.

"I don't know how many cleanses you've done before," she said, "but I can already tell this one is going to be really fun."

John made it through the second chorus before he asked, "Do you have any real music, like John Denver?"

"Ell-oh-ell," Devin said, turning to give me a look that was gently teasing, like *How did you end up with this one?* "Is John Denver even alive?"

"No more cis white men music on this road trip," I said. "Play something motivational. Like if I was walking up to bat, what would be my song?"

Devin put on "Wait for It" from *Hamilton*, our favorite, and we sang along to "I am the one thing in life I can control."

...

If you met Devin, you wouldn't know she was sick. Her smile looked expensive. Her complexion advertised good genes. She seemed to genuinely enjoy the taste of edible flowers. If her body appeared beside a headline about how this woman gets it done, you'd click.

When I met her at an entrepreneur retreat, she had a six-figure business as an intuitive eating coach. This was during a period when I would photocopy proof of my income for any scholarship opportunity I could find—I just wanted a break from New York City, my $28,000 annual salary as executive director of a nonprofit organization that was going to end gender-based oppression through public sculpture, and the cage-free egg salad sandwiches that were often the most ethically nutritious food I could afford.

They paired me with Devin as my mentor.

"What's your edge?" she asked. "What are you better at than anybody else?"

"Working," I said. "Relaxing stresses me out."

"You're a total pitta," she said.

"I'm a what?"

"Your dosha. Do you eat a lot of salted cheese?"

"If I say yes, are you going to tell me I have to stop?"

As executive director, my job was to eat salad with rich women from all over the great island of Manhattan, compliment their avant-garde jewelry and trend-driven philanthropic work, and then beg them to come on as sustaining donors for a series of anatomically accurate yet artistically rendered vaginal sculptures. Every lunch ended with me half-heartedly reaching for the check until they stopped my hand. It was the least they could do. No one ever wanted to come on as a sustaining donor *at this time*, but there was always someone else I should *really* talk to; they would make an e-intro and I had to thank them for their generosity before moving them to BCC. My future was an infinite horizon of fine dining in vain.

"I've built this organization that's supposed to be changing the world, but I'm killing myself," I told Devin. "I'm killing myself for other women."

She placed a hand on my forehead like a blessing. Her palm was surprisingly warm and calming. "Your pain is sending you a message right now," she said. "Your pain says it's time to pivot."

I knew a pitch was coming. I should hire Devin as my coach. She'd tell me how much cheese I was allowed to eat (none) and make me text her photos of my treadmill workouts. After her three-month program, not only would I feel incredible, but *I'd look like her.* The last time I was her size, I was about ten years old. The proof of her program was written on her body. I started to sweat, preparing how I would tell this person I couldn't afford the program. Self-consciously, I put my face in one hand, to cover the patch of acne near the ear I always held my phone to.

"Forget the cheese," I said. "The cheese is not the problem."

"You know you don't have to keep doing this, right?" Devin asked.

"No," I said. "I *do* have to keep doing it." Of course she wouldn't understand. While she was selling self-improvement, I was out here trying to change the world.

"Says who?"

"Says me."

"Hold that thought," Devin said. She opened a fresh page in her rococo floral notebook that had likely cost more than twelve dollars, and began writing. After a couple of minutes, she tore out the page.

PERMISSION SLIP

I give myself permission to listen to my intuition.

I give myself permission to prioritize my own psychic space over what other people want from me.

I give myself permission to decide when it's time to walk away.

Devin's handwriting was as tiny and perfect as a font, the product of years of practicing her uppercase I's.

"Now all you have to do is sign it," she said.

I had so thoroughly braced myself to say no to her that I felt defensive about her reframe.

"But what if my true calling is to ignore my intuition and put myself last?" I joked.

"Uses humor . . . as coping mechanism," Devin recited, as she wrote it down.

"What about you?" I said. "What's your coping mechanism?"

"For me, I find intense physical activity to be really grounding."

I thought that sounded like horseshit, but I signed the permission slip so I could ask her to help me with my bigger problem, which was convincing women like her to give me money.

Devin seemed so perfect that I became obsessed with finding out what was actually wrong with her. That night, back in my hotel room, I installed a new WordPress theme on the nonprofit website to meet Devin's aesthetic requirements, and I opened YouTube in another tab, so I could watch and rewatch a video of her slowly eating half an avocado with a tiny souvenir spoon as I tried to figure out what was so sad about how much she savored each bite.

I binged on all her social content: her YouTube channel, her Insta, her recipe blog. The story she told her followers was that she had recovered from an eating disorder and from her perfectionism and her mission on earth was to help others do the same. She posted Love Yourself memes to inspire women to do what I suspected she was incapable of, like maybe that love would travel in a game of telephone and one day make it back to her, in a form she was capable of understanding. Everyone seemed to be buying what Devin was selling except Devin herself.

I thought I could be the girl sitting next to her in the telephone circle, the one to whisper the message, the smart friend who would help her see how much more she could achieve professionally if she redirected all the time and energy she devoted to controlling her body.

We spent all weekend together at the retreat. Periodically, a fan would come up and ask to take a selfie with Devin and she would happily pose (always on the left—her good side). Everyone knew Devin Avery. I kept telling her it was okay if there were more important women she needed to talk to; I could graze at the Luna Bar buffet and wait for someone to try to network me. But Devin insisted there was no one else she needed to spend time with.

Between her platform and message, and my vision to help women on a global scale, we brainstormed what a self-care social network might look like. It might have remained just a bunch of random ideas scribbled in a notebook except that Devin's dad died and she had the cash to hire a developer. I resigned from my nonprofit with a gust of relief. I started saying, *This will work, trust me*, to Devin and to John, even before I believed it was true. It was too late to go back.

We had a hundred thousand users by the end of our first week. One million by the end of 2016. We moved from two desks at a coworking space in an old button factory near a toxic canal in Brooklyn to renting an office for a staff of twenty (with room to grow) in Flatiron. The election was a gift to us. So was the cover story in *Fast Company*: "Paltrow, Meet Steinem: How Millennials Devin Avery and Maren Gelb Are Making Wellness Woke."

...

There was no traffic on the two-lane road, bordered by bare trees, that cut through a rural county I imagined had once been Native land, before assholes like me came and stole it. We passed gas stations and farms, a cemetery and a vacant baseball diamond, parcels of land with fading "For Lease" signs. Leaving New York was always a reminder of the millions of people who would never choose your life or your lifestyle, the one you fought so hard to have, to prove how special you were.

"Oh hell no," Devin mumbled, staring at her phone.

"What?" I said, my pulse quickening in a way that was so familiar it almost felt good.

"Nothing," she snapped. "You don't need to worry about it." She flipped her phone horizontal and started typing furiously.

Without thinking, I pulled my own phone from my FiveThirty-Eight tote so I could follow along. Did we get a wave of account deactivations? Were women talking about my tweet on Richual? Maybe Elizabeth Warren or Hillary Clinton or Sarah Silverman posted something in my defense on Twitter and now people were piling on *them* and that's why Devin was outraged.

When I unlocked my home screen, I was reminded that Devin had removed Twitter, Instagram, Facebook, Messenger, Snapchat, Slack, my work email account, and even my Richual app. This was the digital detox deal we'd made. I admitted I was powerless over social media and that my life had become unmanageable and surrendered myself to Devin's higher power. Now my phone was brain damaged, as useless as a floppy disk.

I'll download Richual later at the house, I thought, *just to check. And then I'll delete it again. If there's wifi? Will there be wifi?* I'd forgotten to ask Evan. *Shit*. By this point, I wasn't even chasing a good high, just the dopamine jolt I'd get from knowing what people were saying behind my back, followed by the righteous indignation that they were all wrong.

"Almost there," John said, reaching back with his right hand to squeeze my knee. It was startling how much gray there was in his hair at only forty-one. So much of the time we spent together was at home, in the evenings, in the yellow lamplight or in front of the indigo glow of our screens, pale human blobs eating takeout adjacent to each other on the couch. I hardly ever saw his face, and he hardly ever saw mine. Closing my eyes, I could picture him more clearly by recalling the images I'd committed to memory—the boyishness that attracted me to his dating profile years ago, his snub nose and full lips, the tiny space between his two front teeth that he tried to hide by never smiling. The ten-year age difference had never really bothered me because, irrationally, I kept thinking that as I got older, the gap would close. But I remained somehow the "girl" in *girlfriend*.

"Do you mind pulling over at that liquor store?" I asked.

Devin turned around in her seat. "I thought we talked about doing this cleanse together?"

"Is wine not a liquid?"

She sighed in a way to let me know she was now going to do her "breath work." I calculated how many bottles of wine I'd need to get through the weekend. I could hide one or two in my tote bag, and carry the rest in a shopping bag. I could say I was leaving the best bottle for Evan's parents as a gift. I could say, "I got enough for everyone," even though I was the only one who drank.

• • •

The old house was dark and imposing from the road, elevated on a grassy plot bordered by a low stone wall, miles from the nearest village. Square windows wrapped around the brown-shingled exterior like the panes of a lantern. There was no light inside. The house and the garage and the barn were all on different levels, connected by uneven shale paths and obscured by shrubs and shadows, so it was hard to tell how big the house was, but it was at least two stories with an attic, the roof peaked and topped with a chimney. A single light had been left on for us, above the yellow front door.

We'd spent too long at Evan's apartment and the daylight was fading around the edges, but our legs needed a stretch, so we walked around back. Tall evergreens surrounded and shaded the house, and the yard pitched downhill, becoming a large grassy meadow with a pond the color of slate. The grass was dead and straw-colored. A damp red hammock hung motionless between two barren trees. Behind us, a dark tarp dusted with snow covered the swimming pool. I took a deep breath of the crisp bitter air. It was like entering the setting from the gothic novels I loved as a little girl: orphan gets sent to bachelor uncle, mysteries ensue on his estate.

"Stand right there," Devin said. I was on the front porch, pulling the key ring from my bag. She snapped a picture and narrated
the caption aloud, "Hashtag Victorian . . . rest . . . cure . . .
hashtag bae."

I staggered into the dark entryway, putting my hand out to
reach for anything that might be a light switch. Before my eyes
could adjust to the dark, I banged my shin into the corner of
something cold and sharp that clattered when I touched it.

"Fuck."

From behind, John shined his iPhone flashlight at the floor
near my feet. I'd walked into the fire poker stand. "Technology is
our friend," he said.

"You're telling me!"

"Poor Maren," Devin said. She proceeded to turn on all the
lights and open the curtains.

Rolling up my pant leg, I was confronted with the fact that I
had not shaved my legs since the Obama administration. My shin
was scraped, but not bleeding. We were standing in the living
room: a few wrought-iron floor lamps, a wood-beamed ceiling, a
white wicker sofa with upholstered cushions patterned with
strawberries, and a large brick hearth for cooking children in
fairy tales. Evan's taste was futuristic compared to the Mary En-
gelbreit cottage aesthetic and wooden duck decor of his family's
manor. John dusted off one of the mallards and held it up for a
better look.

"Homey," Devin declared, satisfied.

It took me a couple of minutes to recognize the familiar smell,
almost like popcorn, of historic homes I'd visited as a child. I was

pierced by the memory of a tour guide in a period costume bend-
ing down to tell me how privileged I was to not have to spend all
day gathering pails of water that were most likely contaminated
with cholera-inducing bacteria.

Through the living room, there was a dining room decorated
with nautical wallpaper and framed oil portraits of Evan and his
siblings Josh (director of audience acquisition at a chain of elite
concierge medical providers in the tristate area) and Zack (single
dad of a toddler named Walter [as in "White"] and ringleader of a
self-sustaining Libertarian enclave in the Green Mountains).

"Oh my god, look at baby Zack," Devin said. I knew that she
and Zack had hooked up in college, and I'd traveled deep enough
into her Facebook photo albums to know what she looked like
back then, which was shockingly average, like so many other
sophomores, with bodies bloated by beer and Doritos. She once
had rosy apple cheeks and a silly, unpracticed smile. You couldn't
tell Devin today that anything she was doing wasn't working because the evidence proved the opposite true: she had tamed her
body through her will and now she was the face of a startup with
a multimillion-dollar valuation.

"We had sex here once," she said, still staring at the baby por-
trait. "In the outdoor shower. It was weird."

"I'll bring in the bags," John said.

"Come on! I'll show you the master." Instead of leading the
way, she stood behind me and put her small pinkish hands over
my eyes. I climbed the stairs, gripping the dusty banister, until
she said to stop and swung me around by my shoulders, like we
were playing Pin the Tail on the Donkey.

It was the biggest bedroom I'd ever seen, a room that would qualify as a studio apartment in Manhattan. The only downside was the wallpaper—an ugly pattern of green and orange and yellow flowers and flourishes, clustered in a way to look like waving pineapples or, if I squinted another way, disapproving owls. It made the spacious room feel sickly claustrophobic. But there, in the corner, was a huge bed draped with a gauzy cream canopy, conjured by my inner six-year-old. I flopped onto the bed and plugged my nose to keep from sneezing. Devin had her phone out again, snapping pics of the books shelved on the white built-ins as she read the titles aloud to me: "*Women Who Run with the Wolves, Women Who Love Too Much, Women Who Think Too Much: How to Break Free of Overthinking and Reclaim Your Life, Men Who Hate Women and the Women Who Love Them: When Loving Hurts and You Don't Know Why.* Don't plug your nose like that; you're going to give yourself an aneurysm!"

"That's not even true. What do Evan's parents do?"

"His mom's a therapist. Zack said she sent each of them to therapy from the time they were twelve. His dad works in pharma."

"I need both of those," I said.

"Both of those what?"

"Therapy and pharmaceuticals."

Devin sat at the foot of the bed, crossing one tiny leg over the other. "I'll be your therapist," she said. "You can talk to me. I'm being serious! Don't make that face!"

"I'm depressed," I said.

"When's the last time you had your vitamin D levels checked?"

"It doesn't even seem to bother you," I said, wiping my nose on my shirtsleeve.

"What doesn't?"

"Every other day another racist cop shoots an unarmed black man or refugees drown in the ocean or a mother of four is murdered by her husband because she wants to leave—"

"Babe," she said, closing her eyes. "I *know*. Believe me. I get the *Times* alerts on my phone, too. But I wouldn't be able to do my *job* if I got emotional about *everything*. And then what would happen to Richual? It would stop helping *so* many women, right? This is why we make such a good team."

"Because the world makes me cry and it doesn't make you cry?"

"Your job is to cry and my job is to help you stop crying by reminding you how we're leading the revolution by helping women take care of themselves. This is your moment to lead by example, like Gandhi."

"I read something in the *Guardian* that said he used to sleep next to teen girls to test his chastity."

"Fine, don't be Gandhi! Be Michelle."

"When they go low, we go high," I sniffed.

• • •

For dinner, I ate the yellow porridge that was supposed to reset my digestive fire and also my brain. John had a baguette smeared with Brie that he smuggled me pieces of when Devin wasn't looking. I kept the bottle of sauvignon blanc near my plate and told myself, *You're on vacation*, each time I refilled my glass.

Devin told us about a comedian she knew who now had a job writing for a more famous comedian with his own TV show and how it was so great that her friend was bringing more diversity to the writers' room by being a woman, but what would be even better was if her friend had *her* own TV show, but the problem was that she didn't think her friend was very *funny*, actually, because her jokes made Devin feel guilty for being a white woman, as if that was, like, anything she could control?

"Give us an example of one of the jokes," John said.

"Oh, I'm not very good at remembering jokes," Devin said. "Something about pumpkin spice lattes showing up in your DNA from 23andMe. When I tell it, it isn't as funny."

"Is your friend white?"

"What?"

"The friend you're telling us about. She's white? Or she's not white?"

"I'm not saying she was hired because of affirmative action, but I knew her when she had only like eight hundred Twitter followers, so you tell me."

"So you're saying she's black," John said.

I gulped my wine.

"If I don't want to be seen for only being a white girl, I don't want to see other people for only their color," Devin said. "Right, Maren? You didn't hire Khadijah only because she is black?"

"I hired Khadijah because she was extremely qualified to run our editorial content."

"And because you didn't want our staff to be all white," Devin added, moving the wine bottle out of my reach. "Remember?"

"Did you know that Maren is an intersectional feminist?" John said, through a mouthful of bread. John didn't believe in labels. He shared a life philosophy with our user @SmokyMountainHeartOpener, whose profile said, "We're all just humans, being."

"It's not a joke," I said. "What is the point of having those values if I don't put them into practice? I don't want the About Us page to be a photo collage of Julies and Emilys."

"I'm offended," Devin said.

"No you're not," I said.

"And by the way, my friend, the comedian? She's Indian, the country, but she grew up here."

"Well, when we raise our next round of funding, we can hire a diversity and inclusion specialist and then it doesn't have to be just me trying to do my best over here," I said, trying to hide my irritation. "After dinner, let's go over the latest version of the pitch deck."

Devin covered her ears with her hands. "No! No work! You promised!"

"Okay! Jesus. What's for dessert?"

"Gluten-free vegan carob truffles."

"What is a carob?" John said.

"It has three times as much calcium as chocolate."

"I said, *what* is a carob?"

Devin thought about it. "Let me google," she finally said.

John gave me a private look meant to indicate *Why is she the CEO of your company?*

"Let's talk about something fun," I said. "Nuclear holocaust?"

"Rhythmic gymnastics!" Devin blurted at the same time. We

both laughed. Even John had to smile. We worked so many long hours together that it was easy to forget what made us fall in love in the first place. There was the time we were at a networking mixer and I mentioned I had some discounted Easter candy from Duane Reade in my tote so she impaled some Peeps on the rims of our prosecco glasses as a conversation starter. She was a joyful recipient of presents, like the "Nasty Woman" pencil set I picked up at the Christmas market in Union Square, or anything tiny I collected from swag bags at women's empowerment conferences: tiny Shiseido Ultimune Power Infusing Concentrate, tiny Bobbi Brown lipsticks, mini bags of mini popcorn, a travel-size Diptyque Feu de Bois candle. When I had to leave the office to go to a psychiatrist appointment, she'd text me little love notes about how our friendship was one of the best things that ever happened to her, proof of the universe's abundance, and how she wanted me to be healthy enough to share my own sparkle with the world.

More than work wives, Devin and I were sisters.

Khadijah

When I got to the office, it was dark. The heels of my boots clacked against the hardwood floor as I hurried to my desk, hoping to get a head start on email before anyone else came in. Rather than turn on the overhead lights, I opened the blinds over the street-facing windows to let in the sun, but the sky was overcast and threatening rain. That's when I heard chirping behind me—like a ringtone but louder, more persistent.

Blocking the door to the beauty closet, there was a row of glass incubators with eggs inside. Not only eggs but little yellow chicks that had just started to hatch. They were unfurling their wet selves, fluffing and blinking their dark eyes, shocked at arriving. I opened the lid and took out one of the babies, who weighed less than nothing. She curled up and went right to sleep in my palm.

"You weren't supposed to do this."

Maren was standing in the doorway to her office, typing

something on her phone. I realized I was wearing a crop top, my bare midriff exposing me.

"I thought you were in Connecticut," I said.

"Obviously not." She climbed atop her ergonomic desk chair and held her phone high above her head. Then she closed her eyes and threw it at the floor, hard, shattering the screen into a cobweb of tiny shards.

While I wasn't looking, the chicks had somehow gotten loose from their incubators, and now they were running around the office. I was terrified I would accidentally step on one, or that they'd land their fragile feet on glass.

The bird in my palm stirred in her sleep and I cupped my other hand around her like a shield.

"I'm sorry," I told Maren. "I'll put them all back. I promise."

But she wasn't listening. Maren was kneeling on the floor, eating the sparkly black shards like a dog.

"Self-care is putting yourself first," she said quietly, dark blood rimming her split lip.

When I jolted awake, I checked my Fitbit: 4:52 a.m. Heart rate 107 bpm.

I promised myself I'd talk to Maren last week, but it never seemed like the right time and now she was at a Devin-sponsored healing retreat in the woods. Each passing day gave me another excuse to wait, but my relief sat next to mounting unease, like staring at the subject line of an email you'd rather die than open.

I had two tunics that still fit, one pair of maternity jeggings with a black waistband that stretched as high as my underwire.

There were a couple of dresses I once wore with belts that I now wore like sacks, with flat shoes. Most days I wore a headscarf and loud lipstick to draw attention away from what was happening below my neck.

My pitch was practiced. Richual could be doing more to reach pregnant and postpartum millennials. I designed a mock-up for a new content vertical. "This is about teaching self-care to the next generation, building a movement beginning with babies," I'd say.

But what if Maren was like, *How are we going to launch a new content vertical if you're out on maternity leave? What if you just work from home three days a week?*

Or, *I thought we were friends. Why didn't you tell me you wanted to have kids?*

I had fucked up. I'd made myself too indispensable.

...

I met my first boyfriend on BlackPlanet when I was fourteen. *Hey girl, just dropping by to show some love*, he wrote in my guestbook. It was the summer I listened to "If I Ain't Got You" on repeat, the perfect soundtrack for catching feelings. I didn't even care that he'd posted the same thing in a dozen other guestbooks. There was someone out there who wanted to know what I had to say. Little Khadijah couldn't have seen it then, but she was preparing for her future career as an internet writer, using all her available free time to type her thoughts into little boxes for strangers to read. This is when she first started to look at her life—embarrassing moments involving period blood, totally justified rage over who got the solo in choir, the joy of a major H&M haul on a limited budget—as potential content.

I memorized the boy's page on the Planet and consulted with my friend Ashley, who could vouch for him IRL because his family went to the same church as hers. Exactly once, I saw him, in the stands at a basketball game. *Hey*, we said, like we'd been practicing our inflection. But we hadn't rehearsed any words to come after.

It made zero sense that he held the title of "first boyfriend" in my mental archive. More like he was the first guy whose digital attention set too high a bar for future face-to-face contact.

I deleted my page on the Planet once I realized there were other ways to be online, where I could write beyond the borders of a profile. On a blog, you could exist through lists and opinions, ideas about the world and your place in it as informed by Erykah Badu lyrics, good poems by June Jordan, bad poems by you. You could change your avatar. You could stop wearing your old clothes when they no longer fit or went out of style.

I grew up in New Jersey, but I came of age on the internet. I started and abandoned blogs, went through a Tavi Gevinson phase where I meticulously documented my outfits (without ever showing my face because I was self-conscious slash paranoid a family member would find my blog), and then a vegan phase where I made a Tumblr to promote awareness of black vegan celebrities and share recipes and data from PETA.

By the time I was in college, it wasn't enough to make something online. If what you made was any good, people wanted to know who the maker was: "About Me." I watched as the self became what you made. You linked your Facebook and Instagram and Twitter accounts. You were the sum of every vacation photo ever taken, the quantity of birthday wishes you received, the amount of followers you could count across platforms. There was no such thing as IRL. Your body might sleep, but your profile stayed up all night like a lit marquee.

About Me: Khadijah Walker, digital girl in a digital world.

For my gender studies class at Rutgers, I started a new Tumblr called *The Panopticon*, where I documented what I saw to be the prison of personal branding that put women in their own private cells (their social media profiles), under constant surveillance to remain beautiful (but real), strong (but vulnerable), unique (but authentic), vocal about their beliefs (but only the ones that everyone else agrees are worth believing in). We were both the prisoners and the guards.

I posted screenshots of accountability coaches and fitness influencers and YouTube stars and aspiring rappers and moms and women who were "just on this personal journey called Life," leaving vital information, like follower count, but blurring their identities. I made collections of screenshots of women who were all told *stay in your lane.* Another series on accusations of being *fake.* For every mom with tens of thousands of fans for her cute kid photos, there were hundreds of haters who said she was a human disgrace. Being a guard was irresistible.

The Panopticon went viral and that's when the internet became my job.

By the time I graduated, I was writing about women and digital culture for *Jezebel* and *The Hairpin* and *The Toast*. At night, I waited tables at a vegetarian restaurant in the East Village and wrote weird headlines as they came to me on the notepad I used to take orders. The next day, I'd crank out a couple of thousand words to match. "The Best Worst Time I Had Having My UTI Mansplained to Me on Reddit," "I Met My First Boyfriend on BlackPlanet and You Won't Believe What Happened Next," "Questions I Would Like to Ask the White Women Re-creating the Antebellum Lifestyle on Instagram." My regular column was called "What I Regretfully Googled This Week." Lena Dunham DM'ed me in 2013 and asked if I wanted to get lunch, and I kept blinking at the screen, thinking it must be a joke, and never responded. I did screenshot her invitation and made it the header image of my social media profiles. BuzzFeed offered me a job on their social team, and within three months I was a staff writer.

My only hobby had become my career. Every day, I scrolled until my eyes blurred, searching for the next Doge, trying to come up with a hot take about the most highly funded potato salad Kickstarter in world history.

The dudes I met on dating sites googled me before a first date. They had formed an opinion about who I was hours before they asked if I wanted to Venmo them for my grain bowl. "I thought you'd be taller," one said. "Are you going to write about us?" another asked, as if there was ever going to be an "us" to write about.

I wanted to find a DeLorean that would take me back. Naming myself as the creator of *The Panopticon* was the mistake that made me known. What would I do once I had plundered every mortifying moment of my youth for a personal essay? What was left for me to say about how women constructed their identities online? I wanted to escape myself; at the same time I wanted to level up. I watched as the girls I was blogging with at twenty-two were offered staff positions writing about pop music and millennial culture at *The New Yorker*, or about the intersection of race and tech at the *Times*. What, was my meme beat at BuzzFeed not highbrow enough? Was Foucault, like, over? I knew what Shine Theory was, but I couldn't help feeling envy and resentment that they had achieved something before I even realized I wanted it.

I was in the waiting room of my psychiatrist's office, waiting to get refills on Ativan and trazodone, when Maren messaged me.

I'm sure you must get messages like this all the time , she wrote. But I'm the cofounder of a women's wellness startup focused on self-care. There's a senior position that I think you might be perfect for. We have funding. Can I take you to lunch?

...

I texted Adam: I had that nightmare again.

I was too wired to fall back to sleep. On my phone, I googled *pregnancy dream baby animal workplace nightmare*. I searched *anxiety bad for fetus*.

I was used to checking email at least once in the middle of the night. I soothed a sponsor who was upset we didn't use the correct transparent png of their logo, and replied to an aspiring influencer who wanted Devin to give her sponsored content opportunities but Devin was ignoring her emails and wasn't there anything I could do? I opened her profile @SurvivorGirl96: only

3.5K followers. The proportion of meal photos to full-body shots was all wrong. **You have to build your following, sorry,** I told her. **Try posting less pics of meat/more of you in dresses on vacation, etc.**

I scrolled through Twitter: tests revealed the nerve agent that killed Kim Jong-un's half brother, Los Angeles religious leaders were creating a network of safe houses for undocumented immigrants, Beyoncé was canceling her Coachella appearance. **Maybe the millions of people who voted to MAKE AMERICA GREAT AGAIN should have their own rally,** said the president.

I woke up like this, by the light of my screen, vibrating with adrenaline.

What I would say to a Richual user in my situation: *Take a break. Take a breath. The news will still be there when you get back.* But I never felt I had the choice. The only coping mechanism I had was toggling between the news and the stress that was actually within my control.

I had started practicing asking Maren for little things. For our most recent feature launch, a way to sync your Fitbit sleep data with your Richual profile, so you and your friends could compete for best sleep, Maren ordered cases of Chateau Miraval rosé. It was just a small party for the staff and some press. I filled a coffee mug with tap water and watched her work the room, refilling everyone else's glasses so she could refill her own. A couple of glasses in, she was complimenting my outfit, like she'd just realized there was a human being on the other side of all the emails she sent. By the end of the night, Maren was stage whispering ugly gossip—that she'd already told me at the last party—about the founder of a period underwear company, as I deposited her into the Uber I'd hailed on her phone.

The next day, I Slacked her.

> Hey, do you have a sec?

Sure what's up

> I was wondering if I could give
> some feedback on the party.

There was a pause.

Sure! Always

Maybe next time we could also have some non-alcoholic beverages for the people who aren't drinking, I typed.

She said nothing. I stared at my screen for ten minutes before finally clicking another tab. Ninety minutes later, Maren posted a thumbs-up emoji.

In bed, I opened the Google Doc called "Maternity Leave Script."

> **OPENING:** Hi, Maren, thanks for meeting with me. Thanks for taking the time to meet with me. I know you're busy so I appreciate you taking this time to meet with me.
>
> Ask her about trip to Connecticut?
>
> Mention lack of HR dept up top: I know we can't currently afford an HR dept, so thank you for . . . But I hope to use our conversation to . . . I'm sorry to bring this to you directly . . . (Don't apologize!) I thought this could be a great opportunity to create a feminist parental leave policy from the ground up . . . (Too didactic) As we grow as a company, I look forward to the opportunity to give feedback on what role an HR department might play . . .

> I remember during my interview how you took out those neon index cards and had me make a pyramid of my priorities and I put "family" and "health" and "boyfriend" and then you reorganized and put Richual at the top of the pyramid and I always thought that was how you were offering me the job, but now I think you were trying to tell me something else.
>
> Slides for new pregnancy and postpartum content verticals. Before or after I bring up pregnancy/maternity leave?
>
> What would Michelle Obama do?
>
> Due date is July 21. I'm asking for six weeks of maternity leave and another six weeks part-time after that.
>
> Worst-case scenario: offer to livestream the birth, a Richual exclusive (hahaha kill me).

Smile!!!, I typed at the top of the doc.

Last spring, I went on a date with a broke grad student I met on Tinder. We went to see live music at a warehouse in Bushwick. "Honestly I don't know if this is going to be any good," he said as we were walking over. "But bad can be interesting."

So I studied the bad music like a hard-to-parse text. The drummer wasn't listening to the lead singer or the singer wasn't heeding the drummer's lead. The bassist was in his own zone, stoned. The white singer had an ugly, scratchy voice. In the middle of one song, the musicians stopped after the second chorus and the singer yelled, "We haven't finished writing the next verse, so we'll end it there. Good night!"

That was Adam.

While my date got me another plastic cup of cheap wine, I watched the sweaty musicians congratulate each other. Their joy was something they created, by making up words to go along with a loud noise that only they could appreciate. It was hard to imagine a female singer ending a set because she hadn't finished writing all the words to her song, but at the same time I admired their arrogance, their lack of self-consciousness.

"Bad, right?" my date said.

"Ugh." I held the cup to my forehead like I was cooling a fever.

The second time I saw Adam was at a barbecue in June. His voice was familiar even before I recognized his ruddy cheeks.

"I think I might have seen your band play," I said.

"Terrible, right?" He answered his own question with his laugh.

"So what do you do," I said, "besides . . . sing?"

"I'm a carpenter."

I thought about saying something about Jesus but that seemed too obvious.

"When you tell people that, do they ask you to come over to their apartment and fix their cabinets?" I asked.

"What's wrong with your cabinets?"

I cringed. The door to the bathroom medicine cabinet had been broken for as long as I'd lived in my apartment. My roommate and I just kept it on the bathroom floor, leaning up against a wall, mirroring our feet when we stepped in and out of the shower.

"Nothing," I said.

"You're definitely not asking me to come over to your apartment."

"Uh, no."

The skin on his shoulders was freckled and sunburned, stenciled in the shape of his retro yellow tank top that bore Lionel Richie's face and the word "Hello." I would have swiped left. And yet, I gave him my number, to enter into an old flip phone. When I got home that night I searched for him online and found his band's website, but he had no Facebook profile, no Twitter handle, no LinkedIn page. It was like he didn't exist outside the moments we spent together in the same room.

Adam had a navy Volvo wagon, manual transmission, with a hatchback for hauling band gear, materials, and the custom furniture he built at a workshop in Gowanus. After work and on weekends, Adam gave me something better to do than stare at a screen.

We went for drives. My eyes reacquainted themselves with distance. There was another New York that existed aboveground, at the speed of a car and not a bus, Manhattan's fairy lights throwing gold against the starless sky. There were pockets of the city you could only get to in a car. On an unusually cold and drizzly summer day, we drove to Fort Tilden with a couple of bodega sandwiches and sweaty bottles of Red Stripe. No one else was at the beach and Adam went skinny-dipping in the ocean, while I stood on the sand, still in shoes and socks, clutching a folded umbrella.

To be with Adam was to be constantly trespassing beyond the borders of what I thought was appropriate. It was wild to watch how much another person could get away with, just because he'd spent his whole life in skin a different color than yours. Adam was five-and-a-half-feet tall, same as me. He wasn't the first white guy

I'd dated, but he was the first one who didn't automatically abbreviate my name to "K."

The more time I spent with him, the more—this sounds unbelievable, but it was the summer of 2016 and everything was unbelievable—I felt his magic rubbing off on me. There was the New York you knew from movies and then there was the real New York. Real New York was mysterious wet drips on your head when you walked under scaffolding, the blackened soles of your feet in summer, the gust of wind from the subway tunnel that made the hem of your skirt fly toward your chin, how frequently you passed young women crying into their cell phones, blowing their noses on deli napkins. Adam bridged the gap between the cinematic and the real.

When we were together, nothing bad seemed to happen. Parking spots appeared wherever we went. The subway car arrived just as we got to the platform. At a crowded brunch spot, Adam mentioned to the maître d' that he was a friend of "Michael's" and we were seated right away; when I asked who Michael was, he said, "Lucky guess." Outside the Brooklyn Museum, a little light-skinned girl with braids and pink barrettes ran up to us and handed me a yellow rose before running away, laughing at her own private joke.

All I had to do was take one pink pill at the same time every night, but the sticker with the days of the week fell off and got lost at the bottom of my purse, and instead of looking for it, I told myself this isn't rocket science, just take one pill and then another.

In September, I had lunch with Maren.

"I hope this doesn't make me sound like a crazy stalker," she said, "but I've been following you for a long time." She knew I was vegan and had asked Devin to recommend a restaurant, called XYST.

Maren was wearing a slightly wrinkled black blazer over a white T-shirt. She carried a canvas WNYC tote. She used to work in the nonprofit sector, she said, trying to end gender-based oppression by placing sculptures of vaginas in high-trafficked public areas, but she realized the greater impact she could have with a for-profit venture. Maren had a dark intensity that was compelling, but also a little wack, like Aubrey Plaza's character on *Parks and Rec*.

"Every brand tells you they're changing the world," she said. "But has anyone thought of changing the world by actually giving women a break?" She handed me her phone and let me experience Richual for myself, scrolling through all the varieties of self-care, stumbling upon nutritionists and sober life coaches and professional cuddlers.

The platform was ready to launch, but she needed someone to be in charge of all the content, both editorial and branded, to keep users signing in on a daily basis. I'd never been an editor before, but she promised me I'd have freelancers and interns at my disposal. I wouldn't have to write about myself—unless I wanted to. The starting salary was higher than what I was making at BuzzFeed and she was offering one point of equity in the company.

"If we grow to even a fraction of the size of Instagram or Facebook? That equity share could be worth millions someday."

I was twenty-six years old, eating twenty-two-dollar wild mushrooms with kale polenta, thinking, *I bet they don't even eat like this in the Condé Nast cafeteria*, already mentally rehearsing the *so much gratitude for my work family* post I would write when I gave notice at BuzzFeed.

"I'll have to think about it," I told Maren.

At the table next to us, a white woman with dreads was explaining to her bald lunch date why Hillary's Wall Street connections were a bigger deal than Gary Johnson not knowing what Aleppo was. In the car, I recounted the whole scene for Adam, climaxing in an impression of her speaking to management at Whole Foods, demanding justice for collard greens, marginalized at the expense of kale. That made him laugh hard enough he hit the steering wheel like a drum.

We kept saying "anything could happen," but secretly we were sure we were right: Hillary would win. We stayed afloat on our stupid hope.

I asked Maren for 5 percent equity. She offered 2.5 and I accepted and celebrated in my cubicle by listening to Drake and watching videos of golden retrievers on skateboards.

I swallowed the white placebos. One, two, three, four. My period usually came on three. Four at the latest. After four, you start a new pack of pink. One, two, three, four.

Still no blood.

Adam drove us across the Brooklyn Bridge and looking up at the arches though the windshield, I started to cry. "It's so beautiful," I said. He reached over to squeeze my bare knee.

That was the first night it really felt like fall. Adam hated air-conditioning and liked to sleep with the window open. I said I was too cold and he tucked the sheet around me tight as a strait-jacket.

"Still cold."

He rubbed his hands up and down my arms, kissed my forehead.

"Okay?"

"There's something I have to tell you," I said.

"There's something I have to tell you, too."

"You first."

"I said I'd go upstate for a few months," Adam said, "to help my friend Oscar build his tiny house."

I didn't know how afraid I was until he said that. "That's cool," I said, and turned my back to him in bed.

"That's *cool*?" he said, and tried tickling under my arms.

"Stop," I snapped. "Don't. Tiny houses? Seriously?"

"Here we go," he said.

"They're upper-middle-class mobile homes." I couldn't remember where I read that online, but it came out of my mouth like I was an internet recycling machine.

"I've known Oscar since second grade. What's the big deal?"

"I'm pregnant," I said.

For a second, we were both frozen. I waited for him to exhale, say, *That's too bad*, and offer to drive me home. I wondered how many abortions were paid for with Venmo. I was already planning how I would turn this moment in my life into content: "The Best Worst Time I Had Being Impregnated by Jesus's Doppel-gänger," "Seven Misconceptions About the Class Politics of Tiny

Living," "To Celebrate Our First Female President I'm Having a Baby and She Fucking Better Be a Girl."

Then Adam started singing, "Baby, baby, where did our love go?" in his rough, funny voice, wrapping his legs and arms around me in a trap, and that's when I decided I could make this work. All I had to do was work harder than anyone else. If Richual succeeded, a piece of that was mine.

Maren

On our first night in the country, I slept for fourteen hours. Our apartment building in Brooklyn was in the LaGuardia flight path, which added another layer of noise to the normal cacophony of street traffic, sirens, and drunk proclamations of "But, baby, I love you!" when the bars closed at four. We usually slept to the sound of a white noise app on my phone that cost $9.99 for unlimited hairdryer or vacuum cleaner, forest at dusk or womb.

John was already working at the kitchen island. "You slept through the birds," he said.

"What birds?"

Without raising his eyes from his MacBook, he gestured at the French doors that led to the deck off the kitchen.

I went out barefoot in the cold damp morning. Aside from one weekend in Miami, when we rented bikes to ride along the beach and then I got a phone call to say our servers had crashed because a post about live bee sting acupuncture for depression got too much traffic after an influential MD criticized us on Twitter for "risky mental health quackery," John and I hadn't been on vacation in years. I knew I was unbelievably lucky to stay here. I was hashtag blessed. I watched as a dark bird flew, squawking angrily, from the top of one distant tree to a spruce right in front of me. A second bird followed, either in pursuit or out of habit. When the branch where they perched stopped bouncing, I saw the birds weren't black but midnight blue, with an iridescent sheen like an oil spill across their backs.

"Five in the morning," John told me, and then did his impression of their sound, a repetitive grating call. Nothing like birdsong.

"Poor baby," I said, kissing his head, which smelled like the herbal tonic rinse I got him to thicken his hair.

We still hadn't talked about what I posted on Twitter. Not really. Maybe if I had actually asked him, he would have said that joking about taking down a member of the oligarchy was the least I could do and welcome me to the #resistance. While John licked his wounds over Bernie's loss and what-could-have-been, I (according to him) devoted my every waking hour to building a community of self-absorbed narcissists whose definition of political action was serving as brand ambassadors for the first-ever pubic hair conditioner designed for all gender identities that costs sixty-nine dollars an ounce.

That wasn't totally fair.

There were really two communities of Richual users. Dewy-skinned, Glossier-Boy-Browed, chaturanga-toned young women used the platform to sell access to their "lifestyles" in the form of exclusive ayahuasca ceremonies (millennial pink puke buckets provided) or wine and cannabis pairings in Napa. Some of the most popular posts on the app were of white twentysomethings vaping on yachts or soaking in claw-foot tubs of sparkly lavender potion. Hashtag sorryiwaslateididntwanttocome. These women were digital performance artists; they performed their rituals for other women to aspire to. They meditated for the photo opp: the beautiful shaft of sunlight at the picturesque silent retreat in the Berkshires. Their cosmic smoothie bowls, garnished with chia seeds and dragon fruit balls, elevated nutrition to an art form.

These were Devin's users. Her #RichualSisters. She journeyed with them to the ashram in Calabasas where you hike sixteen miles on one thousand calories a day. If there was a yoga class with goats in the Hudson Valley, Devin would bring her mat. She served as liaison between the influencers and our advertising partners, and there was no one more naturally suited to this role than Devin, whether posing with a glass of low-cal rosé at the launch party for a sweat-proof cream eyeshadow you could wear to spin class, or in culottes against a step-and-repeat at a premiere for a documentary about sustainable food trucks.

I paid more attention to the users who would never appear on a magazine cover. I found a post tagged #selfcare that showed a remote control, a box of Papa John's, and the hand of a white user whose knuckles were scraped from bulimia. Some women shared pictures of their weekly pill organizers or their sobriety coins. @ManicBiracialPixie posted a selfie of getting a sleeve tattoo of stargazer lilies to cover up her self-harm scars. If I was jolted by any of the posts I found, it was only because I'd been culturally hypnotized to think of wellness as a rich, white, skinny, able-bodied woman nursing a green juice.

When I compared metrics between the aspirational posts and the posts that were the most vulnerable, I found that the influencers received more comments, but they were mostly from strangers they didn't follow back, while the posts by women that described assault, abuse, mental illness, disability, or addiction received less engagement overall but from a tighter subset of users, who all commented on each other's content.

I knew the formula for hitting the user engagement jackpot. A hot white influencer had to confess: her life wasn't really as perfect as it seemed. She was broken, too. Her fans thought they knew her so well? They didn't know the burden of secret shame she carried. With the right Brené Brown quote below a #nofilter shot of candid vulnerability—maybe a baggy sweater but no pants, hair falling over the eyes—she could share a story that made her followers feel like they had private access to a side she never showed her friends and family. That's what the internet enabled: the illusion of intimacy. There was a fine line between authenticity and TMI, and the Richual queen bees knew just how much to reveal and conceal of their trauma to keep their followers thirsty.

...

After breakfast, John and I went outside and tramped through the damp muck. I wanted him to tell me that everything was going to be okay, that I was smart and capable and I would figure a way out of this. I wanted a pep talk from *A League of Their Own*, an off-the-cuff recitation of a Mary Oliver poem, or at least thirty seconds of meaningful eye contact in a grove of trees, him putting my hands in his coat pockets to keep them warm.

"I feel like shit for asking this right now," John said, "but can I borrow some money?"

No, I thought. *No, no, no.* Possible to rewind the tape so we could try that again? "Some money for what?"

"I have a back-taxes payment due and I'm not getting the next part of my advance for another six weeks." John freelanced as a ghostwriter, writing memoirs "by" D-list reality TV stars. He saw ghostwriting as a way to pay the bills while his real life's work was a novel spanning two centuries, about the wreck of the *Medusa* in 1816 and the cannibalism that ensued among the survivors, a British couple stranded at sea in the 1970s who survived by eating raw turtles, and a young boy coming of age in a coastal town in the early '80s, alienated from his peers and grieving his dead mother. If he could just finish the nine-hundred-page manuscript, if he could just somehow get a copy to Kenneth Lonergan, he knew his life would change.

Then last year, John had his biggest commercial success yet, with a memoir by a handsome house-flipper, about his transition to life as a single dad after his wife died in a mass shooting. This led to a temporary bump in income (and taxes) and similar assignments. The novel was once again put on the back burner.

"Ask Devin if she'll lend you money."

"I'm not asking Devin," he said. "Are you joking?"

"I don't know, am I?"

"Babe," he said, putting his hands on my shoulders so we were looking right into each other's eyes. I loved his eyes. I couldn't go into my bank of email scripts and send my "politely decline" template to his eyes. "I love you. I hate asking you. I wish you were the one asking me for money."

"I've never asked to borrow money from you." Even when I was at the nonprofit, I would charge groceries to my credit card before I asked for any favors.

"I know, that's my point. You're better at adulting than I am."

"You're forty-one years old," I said. "I think technically it's illegal for you to use that word."

"I'm just trying to speak your language," he said.

We walked down the road until we found a couple bars of cell service, so I could log in to my Chase app to see how much I had in checking ($1,242.18) and then Venmo him a thousand. My money was like my time—it always seemed to spend itself, with little oversight or control from me.

"Everything is going to be okay," John said, kissing my forehead. "If Richual keeps scaling at this rate, you'll be at two million monthly active users by when, the end of this month? Ten million by the end of 2017?"

"The worse this administration gets, the more women need self-care." That's what I would say to VCs.

"Once you're acquired, you can walk away," John said. "You can do whatever you want. We can buy a yacht."

"What if we get lost at sea and run out of food?"

"I give you permission to eat me. I want you to live, no matter what."

•••

That night, John lit a fire and we sat around the hearth in our pajamas, taking videos of the crackling logs that our future selves could watch through the lens of nostalgia. Devin played me a gif of Winona Ryder's disturbingly elastic face at the SAG Awards and then my boyfriend held up his phone long enough for me to take a hit of a *Times* headline above a picture of the press secretary, whose saggy under-eye bags were the consequence he paid for his complicity. It wasn't fair. I wanted to check on my internet, too.

"What's the wifi password?"

"Don't tell her," Devin said.

"Tell me," I said.

"Babe," John said. "It's for your own good."

"I *hate* my own good. Ruin me. Please. Shoot me up. Shoot it into my neck."

"Lawdy," Devin said.

"This is what we do at home," John said. "*Intervention* roleplay."

One of the logs on the fire popped. For a few seconds, no one looked at their phone. I finished a glass of wine I'd forgotten to count.

"This is actually nice," Devin said, stretching her legs across my lap on the couch. "We should do this more often."

"What do you think?" I asked John. "Should we become a throuple?"

"What does Devin bring to the relationship?"

Money, I thought. *She brings money.*

"I have a very positive attitude," Devin said. "I notice how people bring out the best in each other. Like the way you finish each other's sentences."

"I can't believe—" John started.

"—he's our president," I finished. "What else?"

"And how John feeds you pieces of cheese when he thinks I'm not looking."

I couldn't solve the riddle of why Devin was single. I could only imagine that men were intimidated by her: she was beautiful, the size of a stalk of asparagus, scented like an expensive bouquet. Maybe she went out with insensitive dicks who underestimated how many self-empowerment books she'd read. Or maybe dating in New York was the problem: it was like being at an exclusive party with someone who was always looking over your shoulder. John and I were together because it was easier to remain a couple than it was to ask ourselves if this was what we truly wanted.

"Who do we know?" I asked John. "Let's set Devin up with someone. Someone really hot. But also nice."

"My personal trainer?"

"Who's your personal trainer?" Devin asked.

"He's joking," I said. "Have you seen him?"

John stood up. "I'm going to the kitchen now to eat my feelings. Anybody want anything?"

"Please and thank you," I said, handing him my empty glass.

When John was gone, I ran my hand slowly down Devin's shin.

"Now about that wifi password . . ."

"You're sick. Seriously."

"What are the top three qualities you want in a boyfriend? Go."

Devin lay her head back against the couch and let out a dramatic exhale.

"It's not a checklist, Maren. It's a feeling."

"But how will you know where to look for the feeling if you don't define some criteria?"

"I don't believe algorithms make love."

"Oh yeah? Where do you think baby algorithms come from?"

"You know what I mean," Devin said, raising her foot in the air for me to massage it. "You and John are, like, comfortable with each other. But that's hard to find."

"That just takes time," I said. "We'll find you someone."

"You don't have to find me someone."

"You know nothing motivates me more than being told not to do something."

Watching the fire burn and glow and then smolder to cinders put me into some kind of trance state where I experienced time at the same rate it was happening, not sped up or interrupted by the little pings I'd been programmed to react to. I felt almost stoned, only able to think one thought at a time. Devin's legs were a warm equal sign across my lap. John ate popcorn with one hand and scrolled through Facebook with the other, occasionally scoffing

in disgust. Before he could read me the latest offen͏
hand to let him know I was very busy experiencing

"I think I'd like to stay," I said.

Devin was delighted. "Selena Gomez took ninety days off from her phone."

"Let's not get crazy. I just want to take the week."

"So I guess that means I'm driving Devin home?" John asked, actually looking me in the eye so I'd pick up his desperation.

"Quid pro quo, babe," I said.

On Sunday night, after they finally left, I dreamed I was falling from a skyscraper and the only way to activate the parachute in my coat pocket was to press a precise sequence of numbers on my phone except that I couldn't remember the combo and so I kept falling—the touch ID wouldn't even recognize my thumbprint and I knew, I absolutely knew, that the phone wanted a drop of my menstrual blood, to prove my identity, but just when I started to roll the phone into the shape of a tampon, I woke with a jolt from the dream, wet between my legs.

...

On Monday, all I had was time. There were no action items I needed to follow up/circle back/close the loop/just check in on. Khadijah could keep the plates spinning without me. And for all the rest, *let them get my auto-response!* I thought, with a thrilling rush of indignation, especially when I thought of the pushy women who sent emails asking for status updates on things I never committed to doing, or the vague invitations to "pick your brain" over coffee when I was already so caffeinated that my brain was like a fluorescent sign. Why couldn't they read it from a distance?

After breakfast, I didn't brush my teeth or wash my face or put my contacts in. Who would know I hadn't? No one. I pulled a dusty hardcover copy of *Sophie's Choice* from the shelf and went back to bed. Nothing like the Holocaust to put your own life in perspective. I flipped to the first chapter: "In those days cheap apartments were almost impossible to find in Manhattan, so I had to move to Brooklyn." *Those days* were 1947. I reached for my phone to Instagram the passage, before I remembered. Was there a point to reading if I couldn't share it? I willed myself to focus on the next few pages, but it was just the young narrator going on and on about his ambitions. Stingo reeked of white male privilege. Where was Meryl Streep?

Around the headboard, patches of the ugly yellow wallpaper were peeling off, as if someone had stuck their nails in at the seam and pulled. Underneath, there was just more wallpaper, a navy pattern with white swirls and dots.

I could have masturbated to pass the time, but Zoloft flattened my arousal and I looked forward to orgasms about as much as I looked forward to low-cal margarine spray. The most erotic moments John and I had recently shared involved watching the brothel scenes on *Game of Thrones* while we sat next to each other on the same couch, not touching, our fan brains completely disassociated from our bodies. Penetrative sex was a foreign country I spent some time in before the election, a beautiful backdrop for memories. I had no idea when or if I'd ever be able to return.

On Richual, we promoted a waterproof vibrator called the Overachiever that synced to an app to analyze and optimize your orgasms. We ran a popular ongoing photo series, "Healing Crystal or Dildo of Antiquity?" (Khadijah's brilliant idea.) There were products for exercising your pelvic floor and e-courses for meditating your way to an O, sold alongside content about the orgasm gap and what it means for gender equality.

At least at work, I never had to be alone with my own thoughts. If I wasn't writing an email or in a meeting, I was on a video conference call, watching everyone make eye contact with their own image. There was someone Slacking me. *Hey, do you have a sec?* I gave away all my secs, all day. *She was generous with secs* my tombstone would say. As overwhelmed as I felt, I didn't know how to be unflappable like Devin, how to just say no with a smile, have everyone love you anyway.

Be more like Devin, I thought, and it felt almost subversive. A totally radical idea: what if I put myself first the way she did, every single day?

I found a perfect spot to sit on the rug in the living room where the warm sunlight hit my face. I closed my eyes and breathed in long and slow through my nose, out through my mouth, like she taught me. After just a few rounds of this, I could already feel a difference, a silencing of my brain hamsters, a softening in my belly, an unclenching of muscles I didn't even know I was holding. Minutes passed. I counted my breaths up to ten and then started over again at one.

One.

Two.

Three.

Four.

I was sucking oxygen on inhale number *five* when I heard it. The sound came from inside the wall to my right, like the house cracking a knuckle. *Old houses make sounds*, I reassured myself. *Watch your thoughts come and go like clouds, always changing.*

I turned my attention back to the slight rise and fall of my sternum and scanned the rest of my body, noting the feeling of my butt on the rug, the yolky sun on my forehead. One of my legs was falling asleep. *Shit. Should I shake it out? Watch your thoughts come and go like*—oh, I recognized the click and the whir of the central heat kicking in, and the crinkle of the aluminum vent flushed with hot air. That's all it was. The sound of heat.

But then I heard a flutter, like the rustling sound of running a hand through a row of dresses hanging in dry cleaning bags.

I opened my eyes and was about to call John's name before I remembered.

I was no longer breathing. Turning around, I stared at the long white wall that bordered the brick hearth as if somehow the silhouette of the animal might appear, a shadow puppet.

It had to be a bird. What else could it be? The sound of desperate wings was now unmistakable, and I tried to imagine what John would do if he were here, while simultaneously berating myself for using a man as my model for taking action. At the far end of the white wall, there was a pocket door I hadn't noticed before. I had no idea where it led—the dining room and kitchen and deck were all accessible from the opposite side of the living room. How did the bird even get on the other side of the wall? The door must slide open to a den or a study, with windows.

Open the door, Maren. Do it quick! Don't think about it! Just do it! I couldn't do it.

I tried a more psychological approach. *If I were a bird*, I thought, *what would I want?*

Light. Air. Trees. A nest where no one would bother me. If I unlatched the living room windows and turned off all the lights in the room and opened the little pocket door and hoped, would it see the escape route I'd made and fly free?

FluhfluhfluhFRSHFRSHFRSH went the wings.

As soon as I stood up, pins and needles rushed down my leg and I stumbled to the windows, fumbling with the locks and screens until they were all open to the cloudy cold. I wiped the sweat from my upper lip.

Open it.

Behind the door wasn't a den or a library at all but a mechanical closet with a boiler and a metal hutch and pipes plugged into more pipes. There wasn't any bird I could see and then suddenly there was—black—but it flew by in a flash, not out into the living room where I hoped it would go but farther *in*, disappearing into a gap around one of the big pipes that fit into the back wall.

Squinting, I remembered I didn't have my contacts in. I limped closer to the tangle of pipes and found yet another door—this one dark, thick wood with a brass knob, like a set piece from Hogwarts, completely out of place in a utility closet. The house seemed bigger on the inside than it looked on the outside. Disoriented, I didn't know if I was currently facing the road or the backyard. "Everything is going to be okay," I said aloud, faking it till I made it. The light was still coming in at my back, and once the bird saw it, she would escape.

I put my hand on the brass knob and counted to three before I turned the knob.

The door was locked.

I would have to find the key.

Devin

Maren's problem was that she wanted do everything herself because she believed she was better than everyone else at literally everything, but the key to becoming successful is to delegate, delegate, delegate. You have to give people little stuff they can't destroy, before you can trust them with the keys to your penthouse. (Not that I had a penthouse, but it was on my vision board.)

When Khadijah asked if I had any task to give our intern Chloé that she couldn't fuck up if left unsupervised for thirty minutes because babysitting was not in her job description and I said, "Why don't you give her something in editorial?" and Khadijah said, "Because she is barely literate," I said, "We all have different learning styles" and that I'd get back to her after I took twenty to meditate on the sheepskin rug under my desk, the only place I could truly be alone.

After I meditated, I Slacked Khadijah and said just give Chloé a company AmEx and tell her to research the best infused water recipes on the internet, go shopping for ingredients, make ten of them in our kitchen, and then Khadijah could decide which was the best to put in the glass dispenser at the pitch meeting on Monday morning. And get the other intern—I couldn't remember her name, but it didn't have an accent mark so the branding was forgettable—to film Chloé in the kitchen and post the winning recipe to Richual because recipes aren't copyrighted, which was something I learned at my own internship at *Vogue*.

Maren must have forgotten we set up this meeting with Dragg & Dropp because she didn't mention it once this weekend and I wasn't about to remind her, even though it was her idea to source creative solutions to the conflict in our comments section.

I was wearing Paige ultra-skinny jeans in White Fog De-structed wash, a sister wife–style blue cotton blouse with a ruffled lace-trimmed bib from Isabel Marant, and Louboutin suede flats.

We'd hired an emerging formerly homeless artist to do a rendering on the wall of a Kanye tweet that Evan chose: "Do you know where to find marble conference tables? I'm looking to have a conference . . . not until I get the table though." The lemon, lavender, and agave water looked fresh and elegant on the sideboard, with lemon pinwheels floating in the tank. Chloé had also taken the liberty of using the AmEx to buy pink tissue paper garlands that she hung above the windows, and tiny glazed celadon bowls filled with feminist candy hearts ("no means no") to put on the table. She was a Richual fan before she became our intern and it showed. *Gold star, Chloé*, I thought.

I took my seat at the head of the table, farthest from the door. Evan and Khadijah came in together, laughing over something she was showing him on her phone, with Chloé and the other intern trailing behind, carrying little notebooks and pens. Katelyn, our brand director, rushed in, wearing earbuds, typing one-handed on the MacBook she was carrying and sat to my left.

"Did you see this?" she asked. It was a YouTube video of Ed Sheeran performing "Shape of You" on *SNL*.

I could sing the words even when I couldn't hear the sound.

Our receptionist, hot pink Beats around her neck, ushered in Doug and the rest of the Dragg & Dropp team. I still got a little thrill sometimes, seeing the conference room filled, thinking, *You did this you did this you did this.* Thinking, *Don't fuck up don't fuck up don't fuck up.*

"We're thrilled to be back at Richual," Doug said, nodding at a female assistant to pass around black velvet Dragg & Dropp swag bags. Doug was like fifteen or twenty years older than Evan and I, old enough to have bought a Nirvana CD back when that was the only way to hear music, but not old enough to be our dad. He was wearing a plaid dress shirt with an open collar under a navy wool vest and jacket. "Love what you guys are doing with gossip protocols to drive engagement."

"Thanks, man," Evan said, "for noticing."

"And I'm Chloé." She stood up and extended the length of her tiny body across the conference table to shake Doug's hand.

"Nice to meet you, Chloé," Doug said. "Devin, how goes it?"

"Did you watch the Oscars last night? Hashtag OscarsSoRight!" I only got home from Litchfield County in time to watch the final

hour, but what a historic moment to be a part of. I tweeted at
Barry Jenkins, but he hadn't favorited it yet.

"Loved *Moonlight*," Doug said.

"I actually wanted *La La Land* to win," Chloé added.

"Well, you guys, I mean, gals." Doug cleared his throat and
reached for his water. Chloé watched him sip with eager anticipation. "Are we waiting on anyone else?"

"Maren is taking a personal day," I said. Out of the corner of
my eye, I noticed the intern with brown hair taking a photograph
of a lengthy rash on her left arm with her phone.

"Very on-brand of her," Doug said. "So, without any further
ado, I'm going to hand it over to Clementine. Clem has been a part
of our Culturally Relevant Production Envisioning, or CRePE,
team for six years, and is the mistressmind behind such viral IP as
America's Most Winning Wedding Singer, *Amputee Reel Life*, *EDM
Sober House*, and, most recently, *Hit Me Baby: My MMA Fiancé*."

Chloé gave Khadijah a look of significant excitement. *EDM
Sober House?!* she mouthed. Khadijah held up a shush finger.

Clem was over six feet tall in flats and looked arresting in a
crisp white tuxedo jacket with a black lapel and thick round eye-
glass frames the color of ghee.

Chloé had unearthed an *EDMSH*-branded LED flower crown
from her gift bag and put it on. Khadijah physically recoiled. *It's
okay*, I mouthed. I knew Doug loved seeing the impact their
shows had on fans. The lights inside the fuchsia flowers blinked
on off *on* off *on* off *on* off. Chloé glowed. I tried to remember why
she was here. She was someone's boyfriend's cousin? Someone's

dad's friend's daughter? The little sister of someone I went to Barnard with?

Even with Khadijah's help, it took Clem a few minutes to get the presentation on her tablet to sync with our projector. We saw the app she had open: The Mindful Fertility Transformation Project—Lesson 14: Using Self-Acupressure to Thicken Uterine Lining. Evan shielded his eyes with one hand, like she was showing us homemade porn or something. I swatted his leg under the table, and he retaliated by sticking a finger inside one of the tears in the thigh of my distressed jeans, pushing to see how far he could get.

"Sorry about that," Clem said, clearly embarrassed. "This is a safe space, right?"

"Courage starts with showing up and letting ourselves be seen," I said, moving Evan's hand back to his own lap. "Brené Brown said that."

Clem had her slideshow up now. She closed her eyes and took a deep breath.

"We're drawn to drama," she began. "When our ancestors sat around the fire and told stories of the hunt, that was . . . drama. When people stood outside in London to watch Punch and Judy shows, that, too, was drama."

Just then, Khadijah's phone went off. "Sorry, but it's Maren," she said.

"Let it go to voicemail," I said. "We're kinda in the middle of something?"

"She wants to FaceTime. Hello? Maren? We're in that meeting with Dragg and Dropp."

"I know! That's why I called! I got the calendar alert." I couldn't see Maren's face, but I could hear her heavy asthmatic breathing in the cold, as she rushed to catch up. "There's no internet in the house, so I had to go outside to get a signal, but there was this bird—"

"Hi, Maren!" I yelled across the table, gesturing for Khadijah to turn the phone in my direction. "The meeting has already started, so I'm going to ask Khadijah to hold the phone up so you can see the presentation, okay?"

"Hi, everyone! Hey, Doug!" From the tiny screen she waved a mittened hand.

"We're thrilled to be back at Richual," Doug yelled.

"I'm so sorry, Clem," I said. "The floor is all yours."

"I'll just start from the beginning, if that's okay? We're drawn to drama? When our ancestors sat around the fire? That was drama." She looked to the ceiling like her lines were written there. "When people watched Punch and Judy in London, that was drama also. Imagine . . . being in the audience during the earliest days of cinema, when people thought an actual train was coming from the screen and they ran away in panic. Fast-forward to the early 1990s, when we thought it was revolutionary to put strangers in a house together and watch them fight and fall in love and fuck and freak out. I'm referring, of course, to *The Real World*." Clem smiled at Chloé.

"Before I was born! But I've definitely heard of it."

"I think *The Real World* is still on actually," Maren said.

"Maybe you can mute yourself until Clementine is done

talking," I said. Evan squeezed my knee under the table. Was I wrong? Did she have to chime in on everything?

"Reality TV is a low-budget vehicle for delivering high dramatic content to a nationwide audience. And I don't need to convince you of the popularity of streaming platforms. We all know friends who go straight from bingeing *The Fall* to *The People v. O. J. Simpson*. Our appetite for stories of victimized women is insatiable." I noticed myself nodding along, like I knew the words to this song, too.

"Let me ask you this: What if there was *synergy* between the fear women feel walking home alone at night and the kind of content that provides a catharsis for that fear? What if there was a way we could all feel like victims . . . but only when we wanted to? What if I told you the next phase of activating the Richual audience is to *hyperfocus* both our content and delivery mechanism, to *customize* dramatic experiences for a niche audience of consumers who are *in an intimate relationship with their palm-size screens*?"

Okay, she was selling me. Even when I couldn't follow what she was saying, I could follow what she was selling. Clem clicked a button on her presenter tool and the room went dark. All I could see were the pulsing lights on Chloé's head and then, on screen, old black-and-white footage of a locomotive coming directly at us, blowing smoke.

Then a video appeared of a white woman holding a little pot of something and a makeup brush. There was no audio, but otherwise the production value was high and it looked like a festival makeup tutorial. She was drawing radiant white dots from her brows to her hairline, smearing bands of red paint under her eyes, and adhering little white sequins to the apples of her cheeks.

"The data that Maren shared with us showed that there were significant conflict clusters around issues of microaggressions, lack of trigger warnings, ableist language, misgendering community members, and cultural appropriation."

"And fat shaming," Maren said.

"But also diet shaming," I said.

The woman onscreen was topping off her look with an enormous headpiece with a red crown and a spray of brown eagle feathers, turning her head from side to side to give the viewer the full effect. Chloé gave a little squeal and a tiny round of applause.

The tutorial video moved to the bottom corner of the screen and now we were watching a different user, another white woman (her name appeared in the lower third: "Caeli"), speaking. "Dear white ladies," she said, looking straight into the camera. Her hair was streaked in a My Little Pony palette. "My dear, dear white ladies. Can we not? Can we stop appropriating Native culture in the name of looking 'interesting' at a shitty music festival?"

The screen split in two. Caeli was now in conversation with another woman (lower third: "Mia"), whose hair was long and shiny brown. "I know not everyone here identifies as a lady," Mia said.

"True," Caeli said. "That's my bad."

"But I do want to address the white folks who think that dressing up like Pocahontas is equivalent to wearing a Wonder Woman costume. First of all, you just put on a war bonnet, which is something worn by *men* in *some* tribes, by the tribal leaders. Second of all, indigenous people are still here. I'm not a character. And my friends and I aren't dressing up like Jews in Auschwitz for any holidays. Like, who determines which genocides get featured at the Halloween costume emporium?"

Caeli nodded.

My phone buzzed with a text from Evan, Genocide: Who Wore It Better? I covered my mouth to keep from laughing. He was right: who would want to spend their time watching this stuff? I wasn't sure how witnessing two women scold another woman for wearing a costume added value to our self-care community. It seemed like the problem we already had with our comments section, amplified to another level.

Clem paused the video and jumped back in, pitching directly to Evan now. "If you've been following the renaissance of *Teen Vogue* . . ."

"Read it religiously," Evan joked.

"Then you know that cultural commentary is hugely popular among the woke Gen Z demo. Our research suggests that user engagement that once aggregated around FOMO and envy is now more dynamic in regards to controversy and outrage."

"In other words," Doug said, "your most engaged users connect with one another through a sense of tribalism. If I'm a woman, I'm more likely to connect with you if you've gone through the same trauma as me. The positive thinking movements of the last century? Forget about it. Now we want to share our rage over a common enemy: the women who don't 'get it' like we saw in the makeup video."

"Wait," I said, "I thought we wanted to help women feel *better*, right? Like, that's our value prop. We empower women by helping them put themselves first."

"Personally, I love it," Evan said. "How do you see this fitting into our revenue stream?"

I turned to face him directly. I could feel my face getting hot and forced a deep inhalation through my nose. "You 'love' it?"

"Well, the beauty is that this will be Richual-exclusive premium content, requiring a paid membership for access," Doug said. "We'll be able to collect demo data on new subscribers drawn to our revolutionary programming, and we'll be adding value for current subscribers. Maren had also shared with us that there has been some member attrition due to . . . women feeling like the platform is racist or ableist. By specifically courting some of those users and giving them a platform for video content, the way BuzzFeed or Facebook has done, you'll grow your membership exponentially. Our projections indicate you could triple your new subscribers in the next six months."

Evan sent me another text: $$$$$$$$$$.

Chloé raised her hand like this was a classroom. "I'm sorry, but . . . does the makeup girl . . . I mean, does the first girl you showed us, who was putting on makeup? Does she get to tell her side of the story?"

"What side would that be?" Khadijah said.

"I mean, like how she *meant* for it to not be disrespectful."

Doug and Clem exchanged a look. I could read their minds: Chloé was the audience for this.

"Great feedback, Chloé," Doug said, gesturing to his assistant to make a note. "We'll definitely bring that back to the production team if *Dear White Ladies* goes to pilot. I think what we're really talking about here is empathy."

Chloé sat up straighter. "Because what if she just wanted to, like, share her artistry and showcase the beauty of Native culture? And how do we know she *isn't* an Indian? Aren't a lot of people part Cherokee, like Elizabeth Warren?"

"Interesting," I said, careful not to overcommit. "Maren, what do you think about Native Americans?"

"I think you're all missing the point," she said. "The broader and more potentially problematic issue is that many of our users—" And then the screen went dark.

"Ah, the gifts of technology," Doug said.

"Can I say something?" Khadijah asked.

"Please," I said.

"There's already a movie," she said, "called *Dear White People*. It was a big deal at Sundance a few years ago. I'm not sure if this is trying to pay homage or . . ."

"We were not aware of that film," Doug said, "but we will definitely watch it immediately. Is it streaming?"

"And I would want to ensure we're financially compensating the on-camera users," Khadijah added.

"Of course," Doug said.

"We would cast six to eight users for the pilot," Clem said, looking at me, "from diverse backgrounds."

"Devin, we still haven't heard what *you* think. You're the boss."

I'm the boss, I thought. *I'm the boss.* Doug and Clem thought this was a good idea, but that's because it was their idea. Evan heard the words *Teen Vogue* and "exponentially" and was like,

"Sold." Chloé seemed on the fence, but she was twelve years old. What was Maren getting at with *the broader and more potentially problematic issue*? I was hoping Khadijah would tell me why this was a bad idea. I felt, inexplicably, like I was about to start crying. My calming essential oil rollerball was in my bag in my office and all I could do was keep breathing. *Respond*, I told myself. *Don't react. Don't fuck up don't fuck up don't fuck up.*

"I'm not *against* diversity," I said. "But our users . . . they're watching this because . . . ? Because they want to shame other women and make them feel bad? That seems to go against every-thing we stand for. I'm not sure *I* 'get' it."

"This emotional reaction is precisely what we were going for," Clem said, looking directly into my eyes, creepily unblinking be-hind her spectacles. "Have you ever seen that video on the internet of the dog who's reunited with her owner and at first she doesn't recognize him, but then she does and she starts licking his face?"

I nodded, mute.

"Sorry to interrupt, but are we comparing women to dogs in this scenario?" Khadijah asked.

"Of course not," Clem said, smiling softly. "I'm just pointing to the efficacy of emotional video content. We all want to be loved, in the way that the dog loved her owner. And the opposite of love is hate. And the antidote to hate is education. So there's a real opportunity here."

"I'm on board with any anti-racist education initiative," Kha-dijah said, checking the time on her phone.

What would Maren do? She would probably ask for more time to review their projections. She would say, *I'm not sure this content fits into our eighteen-month strategy.* She would want to play a role in the casting process, the editing process. She wouldn't release any of it to our users until she had personally vetted each minute of footage herself. And that would waste so much time.

If I'd learned anything from Maren's tweet, it was that the only thing women love more than being angry is being angry at those who are angry about the wrong things. And if there were a way to monetize that anger? Why *shouldn't* Richual be the first to capitalize on that?

"Let's do it," I said. "Let's make the pilot. Maybe we could call it something like *Stay Woke, Y'all?*"

"I love it," Doug said, flashing me a big smile.

"Khadijah can start a focus group on Slack to find out which users are most angry about what," I added. *Delegate, delegate, delegate.* Then I closed my eyes so I could disappear from the room for one brief moment and gulped down my entire tumbler of infused water. It tasted sour and medicinal, so bad you're convinced it must be good for you.

Maren

I didn't know where else to look for the key. I tried every one on the key ring Evan gave us. It wasn't in the junk drawer in the kitchen, or in any of the little nooks in the secretary desk in the master bedroom. I even ran my hand along the cold dusty mantel, thinking maybe they kept the key near the little closet. Nothing.

My phone ran out of juice during the pitch just when I was about to tell them they were miscalculating the audience for their Richual reality TV show. No one was going to pay to watch women police each other for cultural appropriation or not sufficiently acknowledging their privilege or using an expression they didn't realize was offensive to a marginalized community—not when there were so many places on the internet where you could see that shit for free.

Back inside, I put my ear to the door of the locked room and I could still hear something like rustling pages, palpable fear.

If there was a landline, I could call my mom, the only person whose phone number I had memorized, and she would tell me what to do. But I hadn't talked to her in weeks. I didn't even go home to Wisconsin for Christmas. I was the poster child for self-absorbed millennials, prioritizing lattes and avocado toast over saving up for important milestones like buying a house or having a baby or getting a plane ticket so I could sing the alto part to "O Come All Ye Faithful" at the midnight service beside the soprano of the woman who raised me solo.

As a teenager, I'd focused all my efforts on achieving the academic accomplishments that would catapult me out of the Midwest and into some larger world where I'd discover a career that paid enough for me to support us both. A nagging little voice told me that if I really tried, I could do that now. If I ate like she did (coffee for breakfast, dried beans in bulk, Crock-Pot), if I rotated a set number of outfits (*Marie Claire* called this a "capsule wardrobe"), if I canceled all my subscriptions and stopped going out, I could send enough money home that she could cut back on her hours waiting tables, get new brake pads, stock the pantry. But it seemed like such a waste of New York, to not get to spend any money on myself in the city I worked so hard to survive.

What are you so tired from, looking at a computer all day? I read an article in the paper . . . have you heard of these standing-up desks? She was right; how *could* I feel so worn out from doing hardly anything?

The last time we spoke she'd called to thank me for the prepaid Visa card I sent and I had cried, without meaning to, about how difficult it was to scale Richual at a speed fast enough to justify our $5 million valuation and how sometimes I fantasized about saying, *Fuck this* and walking out, and she read me a passage from the Book of Job. I couldn't leave Devin, she said. Poor Devin. The girl with no parents? The sound I could hear in the background was the squeaky straw in the plastic lid of her cup of Diet Dr Pepper. I realized she saw Devin, not me, as Job.

"Devin will be fine," I snapped.

My resentment of Devin's wealth (*I'm comfortable*, she liked to say) was magnified by my frustration that the majority of the labor she put into Richual was her own self-maintenance. She disciplined her body by working out seven days a week and ingesting various powders I didn't know how to pronounce. Her work calendar had time blocked off for balayage and facials and gel manis that were so artful and time-intensive they belonged in the collection of the MoMA. She paid for monthly access to a meditation studio where she could go take deep breaths in a dark room.

Would I have traded places with Devin? Never. I also knew our duo didn't work without her face and physique. That was the sick bind we were in. I may have resented that she'd made self-care her full-time job, but to our investors, Devin was living proof of product-market fit. She was the woman our users aspired to be.

Until we raised our series B, we had only three months of runway. I could work all day and all night, but what mattered more than my grind was whether or not I could sell a room full of male VCs on me, the genius visionary, lady Zuck. Zuckette.

For centuries, women had been told there was something wrong with their bodies, their hair, their skin, their teeth, their minds. They were sold products to "take care" of themselves. At

Richual, we were no different, except—and here's where my genius vision kicked in—Devin and I were women ourselves. We "got" it. Looking good was an ideal left over from the patriarchy. We were about *feeling* good, and existing as a conduit between the brands that could deliver that feeling and our user base who craved it.

And so many women today felt so *bad*—this demonstrated the value our social platform provided. I just had to convince investors that this platform had quintupled in value to $25 million since our last round of funding, or else we'd reach the end of our runway and crash.

My shares in the company would be worth nothing. My mom's retirement plan, which she called the "M.G. plan" for my initials, would be back at zero.

For the record, I never said I wanted the first daughter to get hurt. I only posted a thread about the multifarious and terrible accidents that have happened at garment factories. A revenge fantasy for the next time she went overseas to perform quality control on a peplum blouse.

. . .

On the phone, Harold of Harold's Wildlife Services had sounded reassuringly older, like a sardonic bachelor uncle who can change the oil in your car, but in person, Harold was my age, possibly younger, which embarrassed me. It used to be that when something went wrong, there was an adult you could call, but now I was that adult. So was Harold. When you needed someone to ethically remove a wild animal from your eighteenth-century manor, Harold was your guy, and when you needed someone to recommend the best happy hour drink specials below Fourteenth Street, I was your guy.

I felt like an idiot. At least I'd thought to put on a bra.

"Thanks for coming so quickly." I shook his hand, which was soft and warm. He was wearing a dark goatee and a yellow beanie cap over messy hair. Harold first put medical blue booties over his black hi-tops and then followed me to the mechanical closet.

"This is where I first saw the bird. And then it crawled through that hole up there near the pipe and now I don't know."

"What makes you think it's a bird?" he asked.

"I'm sorry?"

"What makes you think it's a bird and not a bat?"

Replaying the image of the frail spindly talons I had seen gripping the hole into which it disappeared made the hairs on my arm stand at attention. "Because I saw the feet," I said. *Feet? Talons? Feet?*

"Not really the season for birds," he said. "More for bats. People call about birds when really it's bats."

Harold tried to open the locked door to the next room.

"Oh, that's locked," I said.

"You have the key?"

"It's not my house."

"Can you ask whose house it is for the key?"

The thought of having to explain to Evan that there was a bat trapped inside his house and I needed the key to a room that was obviously private for a reason seemed somehow more ridiculous than just trying to problem-solve this myself. *You're in the weeds again, Maren!* I justified snooping for the key because if I found it somewhere, then it was meant for guests to find, right?

"I guess I was just thinking that if it could climb *through* that hole, then it could come back out here, too. Excuse me," I said, and squeezed past him to once again put my ear to the door. There was only silence. "I swear I heard the wings just before you got here."

"It's probably scared now. I can wait," Harold said, sitting with his back against the wall on the floor of the closet. "But if it is a bat, it's not going to come out here again in the light. Last week I was at a house until two in the morning, waiting to catch one. I've known people, they sell their house because the sound of bats in the attic drives them insane. They can't sleep."

"How does one . . . catch a bat?"

"Nets. A bat can fit through an opening the size of a golf ball. If you don't deal with the problem, or if you block off the exits, then what are the bats going to do? They can't eat and they die inside your house and then you have a bigger problem."

Then we both heard it, the *fluh-fluh-fluh*, fainter now than before, but the sound still made my stomach flip-flop in a mix of empathy and fear. Harold stood up to listen at the door. "Huh," he said. "Does sound like bird wings."

This was the most exciting thing that had happened to me away from a screen in as long as I could remember.

Harold set up a dark green trap, a little larger than a game-board box, and showed me how it worked: seed at the bottom would lure the hungry bird and the slightest pressure on the metal basket would trigger a mesh net to cover her. It wouldn't hurt.

He demonstrated by dropping one of his work gloves on the trap and it immediately sprang closed with a loud snap.

"Call me when you have it," he said, like we were collaborators.

Harold removed his booties and put them in the pocket of his overalls. I followed him outside so I could get a signal to Venmo him whatever was left in my account. It couldn't have been later than five o'clock, but already the light in the sky was dimming to indigo.

After I saw his truck pull out of the driveway, I opened my first bottle of wine. After all, I deserved it. Drinking was the ritual that transformed working into something to celebrate and waiting for the bird was tonight's work.

...

Devin and I were a team. She scouted the influencers and courted them, at expensive lunches with the tiniest portions, over cocktails at Le Bain, at female entrepreneur mixers. To become a Richual influencer, they had to commit to leave their other social platforms behind and encourage their followers to join ours. It was like moving your whole family to a foreign country, but once they built their following back up, we would act like an agency, connecting them with major brands on campaigns that would earn them $10,000 or $20,000 or $50,000 a post. No one was spending their marketing budget in traditional channels anymore. It all had to funnel through real people—successful, hot, popular, inspiring real people.

After they signed their contracts, Devin turned them over to me. I worked on the "real" part. Our average Jane user had to buy the sponsored content—the protein shakes and the wearable posture trainer and the three-step cleansing routine to stabilize the skin microbiome—without realizing she was being sold anything. She had to trust that these influencers were human, as messy on the inside as their followers, only with a more polished veneer.

In my email to new influencers, I wrote:

> Our users join our community in order to learn the sacred
> practice of self-care. Many of them are here because they
> have struggled with depression or an eating disorder or
> experienced a trauma, etc. Beyond offering holistic solutions
> and wellness products, we also pride ourselves on the high
> caliber of influencers we recruit, to model resilience at the
> highest strata of the Richual family. You ARE what has
> happened to you and we want you to feel comfortable
> opening up to your new family about that. Please know that
> your answers to the attached questionnaire will remain
> confidential and will only be used with your permission to
> develop the most engaging content for your new Richual
> profile.

I developed the questionnaire after months of lurking and listening to what our users were already talking about. Have you ever: lost a grandparent, a parent, a sibling, a husband, a boyfriend, a friend, other (please describe); known someone who overdosed; experienced sexual harassment in the workplace; been adopted; been biracial; been molested; been a cutter; been in an abusive relationship (check as many as apply: emotionally, physically, verbally, sexually); been raped; had a chronic illness; been diagnosed with depression, anxiety, bipolar disorder, borderline personality disorder, other (please describe); struggled with addiction to alcohol, pain meds, heroin, meth, cocaine, marijuana, food, shopping, sex; had anorexia, bulimia, or an eating disorder not otherwise specified; had an abortion; had cancer; been bullied; been accused of narcissism; felt like someone was underestimating you; thought about taking your own life?

Incest was out. No one wanted to hear about incest. "Molest" sounded dated—I encouraged them to use "sexual abuse" instead because it was more inclusive. Bipolar disorder was tricky because there was so much stigma around it, so I preferred to let the women who looked the least bloated from lithium post about how we need to break the silence around the stigma. Likewise, it was most impactful to have someone who was a size 2 talk about how she had recovered from her eating disorder and even better if that eating disorder was anorexia because no one wanted to read posts about vomiting or laxatives (perfectionism was more compelling). We had to be careful that ED posts didn't come across like how-tos.

Posting about abuse and assault was encouraged, but influencers were not allowed to name their abuser, not even a first name, not even a pseudonym. We didn't have the infrastructure to handle a defamation lawsuit.

Dead grandparents were boring, but I allowed one post a year, especially if the user had a glamour shot of granny in her twenties she could post in remembrance. It was awesome if one of your parents died after you became a Richual member, because the first post announcing the death always got the most hearts. But for everything else, it was better to look back on something that had happened in the past, a crucible you'd emerged from stronger than ever.

Bonus points if you could reveal something from your past and at the same time raise awareness about trans issues or police brutality against POC or the anniversary of 9/11.

"I want to try!" Devin said. Once I developed the methodology, she contacted @GypseaLee, whose following had plateaued at thirty-six thousand. Her butt looked great in exercise tights, but so what? The videos of deadlifts and donkey kicks had grown stale. Unless users knew the woman behind the butt, they weren't going to believe her when she claimed the weekly delivery service of frozen organic smoothie ingredients fundamentally changed the relationship she had with her body.

I showed Devin her questionnaire and sat in the papasan chair in her office while they Skyped. "If you would feel comfortable sharing that," Devin said. "I know, but . . . that fear you're experiencing right now is exactly the vulnerability people *want*. We want to know *we're not alone* . . . You should *totally* post that with one of the pics you took in the Bahamas . . . I don't think you even need to use the word *rape* . . . 'Assault'? We are pushing back against the assumption that if someone's life looks perfect on the internet, then it *is* perfect, right? Say 'I've never told anyone this before.' That's actually true, right?"

Afterward, Devin gave me a high five. "And I have a surprise for you," she said.

She rummaged through a big cardboard box and pulled out a sample of one of the beach towels we were going to add to our merch shop. In mint green against white, it said, "Every Body Is a Beach Body."

"So 2016, right?" She wrinkled her nose and threw it on the floor. The next towel she pulled out was bubble gum pink with a green fern leaf pattern, soft and thick and silky to touch. It took me a minute to see that the leaves spelled "Believe Victims."

"I thought you would love it," Devin said. "Don't you love it? It's empowering, right?"

"We're going to sell this?"

"We can sell it, but we can also send the towels to new influencers after they complete their questionnaires, as, like, a thank-you."

"But is it something you'd want to relax on? By the pool?"

"It's a conversation starter! 'What does your towel say?' 'Oh, my towel says "Believe Victims." What does yours say?'"

The "Every Body Is a Beach Body" towels were my idea, but Devin was right—that message was stale. As a millennial feminist, I was supposed to be liberated already, fine to frolic the beach in my bikini, no problemo, the cellulite on my ass cheeks a proud mark of my body acceptance and rejection of society's punishing patriarchal beauty standards.

"Victimhood is heavy," Devin said, throwing the towel over her shoulders like a chic cape, "but this keeps it fresh."

When we launched Richual, I truly believed we were creating something valuable to help women care for themselves.

Here, we said, *buy this beach towel, try this ten-step beauty routine, rub this on your chakras, brush your skin, tone your vagina, lubricate your third eye, pumice your spiritual calluses, alchemize your intuition, spend all your time and money taking care of yourself because there's no one else you can trust who will.*

...

Two drinks were never enough. Two was only the beginning. Sometimes two meant happy hour at the corner bar with a woman who wanted to pick my brain about how to leverage her viral tweets about gender neutral bathrooms into a personal brand as a thought leader on the paid speaking circuit and I had to find a tactful way to tell her that as a cisgender woman she should really be quiet.

Or a contact from my nonprofit days wanted to partner on a fundraising campaign where we'd give them free sponsored posts to raise money for girls' soccer academies in Central America and they'd give us the social proof that Richual was Making a Difference.

Sometimes the women who asked me to drinks didn't even have their own Richual accounts and I spent happy hour intoxicated on my own smug counterintelligence, knowing I wouldn't help them with whatever they were asking for if they hadn't even put in the effort to join the community.

I knew there were people out there saying, *Talk to Maren. Talk to Maren.* Part of me wished they would stop. And another part of me worried about what I would become if they did—someone with nothing of value to offer.

After a couple of glasses of watery pinot grigio, I had the clarity and focus to head back to the office and start on whatever byzantine email I had been procrastinating on all day. The alcohol erased any doubts I'd had on how to begin and I breezed through my novel-length directives, with the perfect blend of bolded action items and animated gifs to motivate the team. I never spelled anybody's name wrong. I never replied all by accident. I always CC'd Devin so when she got out of her class, she'd see how I kept the torch burning.

    Cheers,

    Maren

On my commute home, I moderated little flares of outrage from the social justice warriors who couldn't pass up an opportunity to let us know a photo collage of vegan lunches called "Nine Crazy Ways to Convert a Carnivore" used ableist language (*crazy*), or to report a white influencer for racism because despite repeated warnings from them, she continued to use AAVE in her posts from the gym (*she thicc, that's ratchet, SLAY*). I waded into a comment thread about white feminism in which a Greek woman was refusing to identify herself as white and a Jewish woman was joining her, while a mob of others (mostly white) were insisting, "You two are the problem."

When one of our influencers messaged me because she was at the bottom of one of these pile-ons, I told her she had two choices: She could capitulate, admit she was wrong, apologize, promise to never again post selfies she took with the orphans she cared for in Mombasa because now she understood the meaning of white saviorism. Or she and I could go back to her questionnaire, find something from her past that showed that she, too, had suffered, and with a single post we could turn the tides of sympathy in her direction.

I couldn't avoid responsibility when shit went down in the community I created, and drinking was the indulgence I permitted myself. While John narrated, in a voice of numb disbelief, stories of Russian influence and collusion and diplomatic faux pas and decimation of environmental protections, I cocooned myself in my own drama—the Richual arena where self-awareness and a scorekeeping of identities took precedence over engaging with any other world.

I never ate when I was drinking. That would be self-sabotage because food created a roadblock between where I started and where I intended to go.

Drink three was when I really started to enjoy myself. The window between drinks three and four was like a Magritte painting—pale blue sky, a beautiful piece of fruit, the touch of a soft piece of fabric.

After four, I started dropping things. I told anyone who would listen what I really thought about the poor choices other women had made with their careers, their romantic relationships, their gauche social media posts of bleeding wounds that no one, I mean no one, wanted to see. At any moment, I might start crying. One night, working late, trying to undo a paper jam, I broke the plastic tray off the office printer, so the pages flew everywhere, uncollated and uncontained.

"Planned obsolescence piece of shit!" I yelled, even though there was no one there to hear me. I thought that was pretty clever, so I got a Post-it note and wrote:

> *This is a planned obsolescence piece of shit.*
>
> *Khadijah, please order new one from Staples!*

I double-checked the spelling of *obsolescence* on my iPhone so I wouldn't embarrass myself.

I wasn't an alcoholic. Alcoholics fucked up their lives, their jobs, their relationships. I performed drinking like any other activity I was a professional at. Sometimes you needed to know when to walk away, but most times you needed to know when to push through to get to the other side.

Tonight, here in the country, I was on my third mason jar.

There would come a time when I would be able to go on sabbatical from alcohol—it just never seemed like the right time to try. First I'd had to survive 2016, then New Year's Eve (who wanted a sober NYE?), then the inauguration. Then I thought, *Let's be realistic, there's no way I can quit until Richual is acquired and I know I have a financial cushion*, so I held out for that future, a moving target.

I'd done my Google research. I knew that if I wanted to modify my drinking habit, I needed to make sobriety easier to accomplish, and drinking harder. I should not have kept wine in the apartment (I bought it by the case). I should have declined offers to "join in on a bottle" over lunch meetings, but it was too easy to say yes, to perform the role of the fun cofounder, whenever Devin's food issues were most excruciatingly apparent. *Could I just get a hot water with lemon? How is the asparagus prepared?*

Access to drinking was my problem; not *drinking*. When I finished this bottle, there was another bottle to open, right in the door of the fridge, and if I knew the wifi password, I wouldn't be able to resist adding the Richual app back on my phone, thumbing down to refresh, refresh, refresh.

"Access," I said out loud in the bright kitchen. "*Ex*cess. Access *excess* access *excess*." I hardly had access to anything at the moment, but it was usually everything—newspapers, magazines, Twitter, Facebook, Snapchat, Instagram, Street View images of the little white house I lived in as a child, the local weather forecast for Wausau, my high school crush's LinkedIn profile, *Harvard Business Review* articles on leadership qualities, a YouTube clip of Amy Poehler as the cool mom in *Mean Girls*, a trove of Beyoncé gifs. There were few barriers to accessing the tremendous amount of material I could entertain myself with while I avoided facing my life.

Maybe that was the problem. What if there were a better way to control access to Richual itself, to cut down on all the drama, and provide a better user experience? What if all of our assumptions were wrong? Rather than scale as fast as possible, what if we limited our users? Wouldn't people be willing to pay for a more heavily moderated internet? Wasn't that what sucked most about the internet—the lack of any accountability or oversight?

If millennials were willing to pay for Blue Apron, for camp-sites with wifi and prebuilt tents, for wine-of-the-month clubs that catered to whether they preferred the taste of bitter herbs to blackberries, wouldn't they pay for a social media platform where they could share all the things they couldn't say on Facebook be-cause that was where their parents were?

We didn't need premium video content to turn our current users into paid subscribers. We needed a whole new model.

I found a piece of paper and started scribbling:

> *More users = better (NOT NECESSARILY)*
>
> *Subscriptions are free = advertising pays vs. paid subscriptions*
>
> *People value what they pay for*

Self-care is worth paying for . . . We are self-care nation . . . some-thing about putting on your oxygen mask before helping others . . . We are the oxygen in the oxygen mask . . . Do you want free oxygen or do you want . . . Devin could come up with the tagline. She could contribute something.

I had to reach her. We could announce our pivot at the Found-ress Summit, where Devin was moderating the keynote! I was hardly ever in such a party hat/balloon emoji mood. I uncorked a new bottle and refilled my jar. A toast to myself. Then I picked up my phone, only to be cruelly assaulted by the home screen: "No service."

If I were a wifi password, I thought, *where would I be?*

Evan wouldn't want to live in a world without high-speed

internet access. To find the password, I only needed to figure out which room was his.

Past the master at the top of the stairs, there were a few more bedrooms along a narrow hallway, plus another door at the end that led to an annexed wing (or so Devin told me), where the boys' nannies had stayed when they were little.

The first door on the left led to a guest room, with two four-poster twin beds from the last century, where Devin had slept, leaving an unmade bed behind her for someone else to clean up. I tried the room next to it, which had bunk beds and a wooden chest painted to look like a parrot cage.

As soon as I opened the door across the hall, I knew this was Evan's room. The bedding was striped dark gray, more modern than the lace and florals in the other bedrooms. The bedside lamp had built-in USB chargers. Above the headboard, there was a framed black-and-white photograph of a woman's legs dangling off a fire escape. A desk against the windows had a keyboard but no monitor, a Moleskine notebook, a wireless Bose speaker, and a coffee mug of pens. I started rifling through the desk drawers to see if I could find anything that looked like a password. Paper clips, rubber bands, a cell phone charger that plugged into a car's cigarette lighter, a movie ticket stub so old I couldn't even read the name of the movie, just a bunch of random useless garbage. But he obviously spent time here on a regular basis, or else why go to the effort to decorate this room?

When I opened the Moleskine notebook, a single brass key slid out of a pocket attached to the inside cover. *Holy shit!* I'd almost forgotten my bird. She'd been trapped in that room for hours. What if the bird was thirsty? I ran downstairs, my steps making a racket in the empty house, and filled a little teacup with water.

Already, I was mentally rehearsing the story of how I came up with the idea to transform my company's revenue model, on the same night I rescued a trapped animal that represented the flickering hope of Americans who wondered if we would ever escape this darkness. *That was the night I realized everything was going to be okay.* It would make a great anecdote for a podcast interview. Gently moving the bird trap out of the way with a foot so I wouldn't accidentally activate the trigger, I closed my eyes and fit the key into the lock. With a satisfying click, I was in.

All I could hear was the squeak of my own feet on the floorboards. There was no sound of wings. I squinted in the near-dark until I found a lamp switch.

The ceiling was so low, this must have been former servants' quarters. It was now a junk room, barely big enough to hold a black futon covered in piles of plastic packages and cardboard boxes and sheets folded in sloppy stacks and rubber-banded envelopes of photographs. "Here, honey," I said, whistling. Assuming the bird was still scared, hiding, I started to lift and move the boxes and piles and what I found myself holding were cords of rope, a black silk sleep mask that said "Fuck" on one side and "Sleep" on the other, a copy of *The 4-Hour Body* by Tim Ferriss, and a few plastic bags of wigs. There was a "MISOGYNY KILLS" black tank top that I'd seen Evan play Frisbee in once. There were a few vibrators, still in their packaging, that I recognized from the pile of products we were sent to review at Richual. Of course Evan wouldn't spend his own money furnishing his sex dungeon. He'd practice pleasuring women with whatever gadgets were marketed for women to pleasure themselves with.

I had seen too much already. I was inside the lair. I was buzzed enough to open one of the envelopes of photographs without wondering whether I'd crossed a line.

A woman with very pale skin wearing a red wig, eyes closed, lying flat on her back in the bed with striped sheets upstairs, the sheets pulled up to her collarbone, like a corpse. A younger woman with a pixie cut, sleeping on her side with her hands sweetly folded under her cheek, a praying Precious Moments doll. There were more of the woman in the wig but with the sheets pulled down and her round breasts exposed, her stiff nipples pointing right at the photograph above of the headless woman on the fire escape. The Precious Moments figurine, her eyes still closed, with a penis in the O of her mouth. The women looked like dolls—was that his fetish? Evan turned women into his sex dolls?

Before I could finish my own thought, I heard the burglary alarm go off. My heart raced against the cage of my chest—the room was rigged. I'd been caught. I ran out of the dungeon toward the sound: the ringing phone mounted on the wall next to the refrigerator.

"It's me," a voice said. "It's John."

"I didn't even know there was a landline here. You scared the shit out of me." I reached for my wine jar.

"The Secret Service is here."

"The what?"

"About your tweet."

"You're fucking kidding me," I said. I was having a nightmare. That's all. I was falling from a building. My teeth were crumbling in my head.

"They're asking me when you'll be home."

Devin

In the locker room, I changed out of my dusty pink Alice + Olivia button-up shift dress with burgundy piping and velvet pussy bow into a porcelain Heart Opener Bodysuit from Lululemon and cropped Earl Gray Awakening tights with a comfortable high-waisted fit. Using a Groupon to get my pubes laser-removed back when it was still socially acceptable to use Groupon was an act of self-love. Our trend forecasting firm said pubic hair was making a comeback but tell that to anyone working in the boutique fitness industry.

At Pheel, the walls were covered in shadow-box frames filled with gemstone pendant necklaces. A curtain made of fawn-colored feathers hung by jute string from a piece of driftwood next to the reception desk, where Elecktra always greeted me by name and handed me a glass of filtered water, no ice. I'd been coming to Pheel since before they had bottles of Chanel Hydra

Beauty Serum and baskets of organic cotton tampons in all the bathrooms. It used to be just six or eight of us on Tuesday nights in one room of a yoga studio. Then Pheel became so popular that they took over the yoga studio. And when the Weight Watchers across the hall closed, they rented that space, too, and doubled the size. Now there was a merch shop where they sold Palo Santo smudge sticks ("burn what's haunting you or just burn up your Insta feed"), a $495 meditation mat in "bisque," and natural crystal Chakrub dildos in amethyst and jade, designed to "remove blocks caused by sexual trauma."

What was once Weight Watchers, that sad arithmetic of self-denial (and what if you're not a math person?), was now a sanctuary, with light mauve walls and a floor lacquered with a subtle lavender sparkle. After kneeling at the altar at the front of the room, where there were white pots of white orchids, white pillar candles, and a collection of clear quartz for healing, we put our mats down in alignment with little pale purple hearts on the floor that organized the sanctuary into twelve rows of disciples.

My favorite teacher was Tressa, self-identified Scorpio. It was always hard to tell if she was twenty-seven or more like thirty-seven, but sometimes she told the class stories about being a backup dancer for Destiny's Child, which made me think she was even older than I thought. Her lips and cheeks were incredibly full yet realistic, thanks to Juvéderm. The sad part was that her dance career was halted when she got a double hip replacement and she credited the Pheel method with helping her rewrite her own corporeal story, which so inspired me because of how much of our bodily experience is actually articulated in the mind, and if we can alter our bodies, we can alter our potential, and I really believed that.

I saw some familiar faces in the row ahead of me—the blonde with the tight traps who always wore a braided ponytail and a strappy racerback crop top; the older woman with thin hair and loose skin around her triceps even though she tried so hard, she really did, but aging is bodily terrorism; the pretty brunette with the bubble butt in white hot pants that showed off her olive skin.

A woman in black yoga pants covered in cat hair and a gray T-shirt that read "Purdue" put her mat down right next to mine and looked genuinely relieved to see me. She must have been one of my Richual followers, but whether or not we'd met before, I couldn't remember. Her face was already red and damp from having to climb three flights of stairs to the studio and I felt a surge of empathy for this person who was brave enough to come up so close to someone she only knew online, without worrying about her appearance.

"Have you taken this class before?" she asked.

"I've been coming since it was Weight Watchers."

"I've tried that, too," she said, sitting with her legs straight out and reaching for her toes in an imitation of Muscle Back in the row ahead. "But you don't need to lose any weight."

"All those years of having an eating disorder have paid off," I joked, but she didn't laugh. I could understand why she was nervous. She'd heard stories about Pheel. There was a little flutter in my heart center when I realized I could be her IRL inspiration.

Tressa dimmed the lights and the candles glowed brighter. Class started with "The Chain" by Fleetwood Mac, and for the length of the song, we alternated between pounding our heels on our mats, squats, and curtsy lunges. My calves felt caffeinated as they began to blaze with energy. Tressa cranked the volume on "If you don't love me now, you will never love me again," and when it got to the driving guitar solo, we all started running in place and grunting "Huh" on every fourth beat.

RUN RUN RUN HUH RUN RUN RUN HUH
RUN RUN RUN HUH RUN RUN RUN HUH
RUN RUN RUN HUH RUN RUN RUN HUH

"This is your container!" Tressa screamed. "Make the container yours!" I closed my eyes and felt the blood pounding in my ears and all the anxieties of the world beyond my mat floated away, like dandelion fluff.

After the warm-up, the music softened and Tressa told us to put one hand on our heart and one on our belly and feel the pulse of our unique life force. "If you don't love *yourself* now," Tressa said, "you will never love yourself again. Love yourself *now*. Use this container, this space, for love."

Purdue might have been crying next to me, but I didn't open my eyes to look because I wanted to give her privacy.

"For those of you who don't know me, I had an injury," Tressa said, her words amplified by headset throughout the sanctuary. "They told me I would have to relearn how to walk. This was a wound to my livelihood." This was a story I knew already, but I never got tired of hearing it, like *Goodnight Moon*.

"They told me there would be pain," Tressa said. Her voice was scratchy sexy like Emma Stone's. "They said, here, take a pill for your pain. And I said—" I opened my eyes to see her go up into a one-armed handstand against the wall, her legs splayed like a starfish.

Next up was Florence and the Machine and four minutes of alternating side plank and thirty seconds of down dog and four minutes of down dog burpees and three minutes of quadruped hip extensions (single-time and double-time) and then back to re-peating the burpees, which was usually the point in the sequence where I had to summon all my remaining willpower to not throw up, but the harder the burpees got, the louder the music got, and Tressa was telling us to scream and I was, and Tressa said, "No, really, I mean *scream*," and everyone around me was moaning like a primal layer of pain on the soundtrack, like we were giving birth to *ourselves*, and when it was so loud and so dark in the room that I was absolutely positive my anguish was anonymous, I cried out, "I MISS MY DAD," and then I sort of blacked out until I recognized the sex voice of Kings of Leon and I was on my back doing a modified bridge pose hip thrust with butterflies and my glutes were sobbing, but I wouldn't stop until Tressa gave us permission to go into child pose.

"Whatever story you are telling yourself about your own body, about your own capability . . . *change the story*."

In child pose, I sensed Tressa right behind me. She sat and draped herself across my back, spine kissing spine. My knees wide, I surrendered to the deepening of the stretch in my inner thighs and low back. If I turned my cheek to one side, I could smell her, sweet and familiar like cardamom and fig. *She chose me.* I couldn't remember the last time anyone had really touched me, with such weight and pressure and intention, and that made

me literally start crying, face down into the bumpy pillow of my
hands, my lips slicked with salt.

...

At home, I rolled out my yoga mat, lit a row of tea candles on my
windowsill, and made a quick video of going into a headstand
from a straddle—a piece of cake once I was totally wrung out
from Tressa's class, nearly light-headed with the pleasure of emp-
tiness. There was some under-boob sweat on my bodysuit, but
from upside down it just looked like a shadow.

Here's looking at you, kid, I posted in the caption. My dad
used to always say that to me. But then I remembered Maren's
rule about how many times you were allowed to mention a dead
parent. I deleted it.

Shout-out to the special friend I met tonight, I wrote.

No, that made me sound desperate. I never even asked Purdue
for her username.

Inversions great for bedtime, I posted. After a long day of at-
tending to the needs of others and agendas you never signed up
for and eating on THEIR schedule and having to make tough de-
cisions, the universe has a message for us and it's: go upside
down. See the world from another point of view. Tomorrow is
waiting.

Then it was time for a shower. I had a mold-resistant and anti-
microbial chrome showerhead so I wouldn't get cancer. First I
washed my hair with Christophe Robin purifying shampoo with
jujube bark extract and then while my hair mask was soaking, I

double cleansed with Kiehl's Midnight Recovery Botanical Cleansing Oil, followed by a glycolic acid face wash by Kate Somerville. On my body, I used exfoliating yoga soap, made with shea butter and marine nutrients, with an aquatic bouquet of sea kelp and coconut. On my vulva, I used Drop of Hope from Lush, made with rapeseed oil and tofu.

After toweling off and slathering my body in Mojave Ghost body lotion by Byredo, I slipped on a lightweight bamboo jersey racerback nightie. There were 512 hearts so far on my post and thirty-six comments. @PaleOhHellNo said, **You glow girl!** She had twice as many followers as I did and was friends IRL with Kendall Jenner. @SurvivorGirl96 asked for the brand of my yoga mat and I told her. @YOLOFlow said, **Aren't headstands recommended for morning, not bedtime?** and I replied with a shrug emoji, and then @Youre1WildAndPreciousLife wanted to know if headstands are good for people with eczema, but I could not handle even thinking about eczema so I didn't respond.

My anti-inflammatory, gluten-free, dairy-free, low-glycemic non-GMO organic meals were delivered weekly by Urban Remedy. I grabbed a Rainbow Salad from the fridge, with red bell pepper, Swiss chard, pumpkin seeds, roasted beets, kohlrabi, tatsoi, mizuna greens, and arugula, tossed with an olive oil and apple cider vinaigrette with Himalayan pink salt. I ate at my kitchen island, sipping from a dark glass vial of probiotic Gut Euphony tincture between bites, and thumbing through Slack on my phone with my left hand.

There was a DM from Chloé that said, **Love that video!!!** I responded with a heart.

Eating food reminded me I was due for a colon hydrotherapy session and I posted to the #editorial channel to see if anyone wanted to come with me and write a story about it for the site. Then I sent Khadijah a DM to ask Chloé to make an appointment for me at the clinic.

A text message popped up. It was Evan. He said, Hey.

There was usually a reason for him texting me at night and this reason made me hold my breath and so I didn't respond right away, just in case I was wrong. I watched the little ellipses like a livestream from his brain. Thinking about his brain made me think of his neck, the smooth pale skin at the nape, the way he hated if I touched his hair, which for whatever reason only made me want to touch it more.

Are you watching Trump address to Congress?

Definitely I was wrong about why he was texting me. Lol no, I said.

You were great in the meeting yesterday. I could tell you were flustered at one point but no one else could tell.

I wasn't flustered. I let out my held breath with a huff. What makes you say that?

I couldn't help but replay the scene at the conference table in my mind. Was he referencing how awkward it was to have Maren call in? But that wasn't my fault. All I ever did was try to protect Maren. She was so fragile. She didn't need to know what Evan had texted me in the car when we were driving to Litchfield County; she didn't need to know what he said he would have done to me in the walk-in closet if she wasn't there watching us.

Evan avoided my question. Come over? he said.

I didn't respond right away. "Alexa," I said out loud. "Play 'Shape of You.'"

No too cold , I said. Take an Uber and I'll leave keys under mat. My doorman knew Evan; there was never a problem with him getting in and taking the elevator up to my floor. It was better this way, more realistic than when I went over there.

I took the time to blow-dry my hair and rub my face with three drops of frankincense oil from a tiny blue vial. I kept my underwear on and tucked myself under the covers, sealing a letter in an envelope.

Evan texted again from the Uber. No touching.

I'm not , I wrote back. Minutes of prickly anticipation passed, a similar sensation to the one I got right before Tressa's classes, like waiting to let someone else captain the vessel of my body. I wanted to give up control. I obeyed Evan, but even without touching, I was already wet, predicting how our game would play out. I closed my eyes and arranged my arms in an imitation of sleep, my best fairy-tale princess in a coffin pose, an erotic Savasana.

My phone buzzed again. You want this , he said.

I did, but it was hotter to not admit it, and I put my phone under my pillow without responding. Like orgasming in a dream, I could almost make myself come by simply imagining what would happen next: hearing the slow turn of the key in the door and the sound of Evan slipping off his shoes and coat. Knowing he's in my bedroom by the sound of the belt buckle hitting the oak floor. A few last seconds of waiting with my eyes shut as he softly climbed onto the bed, hovering above me like a dark shadow, pulling down the sheets. Up close I could smell him. He dragged the straps of my nightgown down to my waist and watched (I could only imagine he watched) my nipples respond to the cold before running the pads of his thumbs across them. My job was not to wake up. My job was to keep my eyes shut. And this was what I wanted, a job. He smelled my hair and kissed an earlobe, the sensitive skin at my throat, my clavicle, my breastbone, licking down to my navel, and then Evan sucked a nipple while a hand went under my nightgown and pulled aside the crotch of my panties. His long fingers were warm inside me, thrusting and beckoning like a hook. He never kissed my mouth or anywhere on my face. That was not how the game was played. The game was I did not move or make a sound. The game was I never opened my eyes. I remained limp as a doll when he finally removed my panties and fucked me silently for five or six minutes before coming all over my placid face.

So You Want to
Be a Foundress?

Khadijah

Hey y'all,

My name is Khadijah Walker and I'm the SVP of editorial strategy here at Richual. Thanks so much for taking the time to contribute your feedback to this working group, so that we can create the most inclusive, intersectional user experience. The most passionate members of this group may be tapped for future (paid) opportunities, so don't hold back! Let us know where you see problematic posts and why they're problematic to you. You're welcome to share screenshots of Richual conversations or just copy and paste.

NevisFong

@KhadijahWalker thank you for holding space for us to contribute. I joined Richual after the election because a friend told me it was a place where I could just chill and take a deep breath, in between calling my reps, but the longer

I'm here, the more I realize how many posts are women opening up about horrific things that have happened to them. Is there any way to enforce a content warning, so that we can skip those posts if we want to? Thank you for listening. (Sorry so long!)

The_s_is_silent
@NevisFong that is a good reminder to always include content warning! TY!

Felice
@NevisFong @KhadijahWalker maybe there could be a button we could push if someone doesn't include a content warning, to report them?

NicoletteLee
Is there a reason that I have almost 8,000 followers and I've never been contacted by Richual about becoming an influencer? I wonder if there's a bias against women of size with vinyasa practices. I see @SmokyMountainHeartOpener posting videos sponsored by almonds all the time. Am I not worthy of the almond shill? 💀 ⚧

JustDiana
@NicoletteLee I'm one of the Richual interns helping @KhadijahWalker and just want to say I follow all your posts and you should totally be an influencer!

Allison
Can I get a ban on YAS QUEEN from cis straight white girls who don't understand its provenance as a phrase

of resistance in Black drag culture during AIDS
epidemic?

Gili
What if every Richual user put their identity markers in
their profile so we all wouldn't have to make assumptions
from their pic? Like Black, white, Jewish, Palestinian, cis,
trans, NB, straight, bi, queer, vegan, gluten-free, Pisces,
INFJ, etc.

The_s_is_silent
@Gili You should also have to disclose who you voted for!!!

Gili
@The_s_is_silent 👍

NevisFong
@Gili @The_s_is_silent I wouldn't want to shame anyone
who isn't a US citizen (and couldn't vote)

Aja_dontgothere
I think if someone posts photos of themselves at March for
Life, that should be cause for removal. Richual is supposed
to be about supporting a woman's right to choose, right
@KhadijahWalker?

Felice
@Aja_dontgothere Or wearing a MAGA hat.

Aja_dontgothere
@Felice GIRL YES 😂

KhadijahWalker

@Aja_dontgothere We definitely support a woman's right to choose but we also support marching for what you believe in.

JustDiana

When I went to Lesbians Who Tech, they had a code of conduct. Maybe we could have one too! I will start a Google Doc of all these great ideas.

I sent @JustDiana a private message: Please don't promise anything we can't deliver. We are just here to listen right now. I checked my Fitbit and my heart rate was up six points just from following the thread. We didn't care about their ideas for improving the platform. They didn't work at Richual.

Got it, boss, she typed back.

I gave my other intern, Chloé, another task altogether. I want you to go through all our users and see who is on which diet (vegan, Paleo, GF, keto, Whole30, raw, etc.) and make me a bar chart of their ranking in popularity. We had nearly two million users. This task would keep her busy until her internship was over, which was good for me, and she could put that she did "data science" on her résumé, good for her.

It was Wednesday and I was working from home so that I could catch a 4:15 prenatal yoga class. Devin was likely pacing the office, staring at my empty desk space, forgetting that she herself had agreed to me working from home one day a week. *You just have to get through this*, I told myself. *And then you get to go somewhere they make you breathe.*

I bit into a caramel almond Kind bar. If the Dragg & Dropp people wanted callouts and takedowns, I had to get the working group to trash specific users.

KhadijahWalker
Thanks everyone. @JustDiana and I would love to know if there are any users SPECIFICALLY you want to call out (or call in)? @NicoletteLee mentioned @SmokyMountainHeartOpener. Anyone else? When you think "white privilege," who do you think of?

Within minutes, @Allison had shared a screenshot of Devin at a charity gala, wearing a sheer dress with a plunging neckline and a VR headset, looking like the physical embodiment of a flute of champagne. **So grateful to @MarcMoulin for using tech to transport us to Mogadishu. So blessed to be one of the first to experience this transformational tool for compassionate journeys,** Devin had written in the caption to her post.

Allison
You mean like this @KhadijahWalker?

Felice
@Allison A DEVIN AVERY CLASSIC

The_s_is_silent
@Allison This is incredible I've never seen it before

Gili
@Allison Eat the rich 😂

Aja_dontgothere
What about this

It was a photo of Devin wearing a pink hat at the Women's March, standing next to Amy Schumer, as they both took big bites out of street vendor hot dogs. **Hashtag white feminism,** @Aja_dontgothere said. **At least she's eating something! lol,** replied @The_s_is_silent. **Hashtag not all hot dogs,** @JustDiana added. **This is why that man is in the White House right now,** @Gili typed. **Devin represents the 53 percent.**

They were gleeful at the game. It was so easy—anybody could play. There was a post of Devin bragging that her blowout was on fleek; a profile of her in *New York* magazine accompanied by a photo of her posed in bed in a vintage silk kimono; a pic of a steaming hot bowl of pho, captioned "I'm starving," dated the same day that two boats of Syrian refugees capsized off the Italian coast. There were layers of offense to unearth here, and everyone was on an archaeological dig.

Devin made Richual for you, I wanted to tell them. *She's the reason we're even here talking about this.* But I felt frozen, unable to type anything in her defense. Couldn't we talk about users who wore so much bronzer it bordered on blackface? Or what about how all the influencers opening up about their eating disorder recovery were white, as if EDs didn't also impact WOC? If I said, *Not Devin, name someone else*, they'd call me Uncle Tom.

I was back inside *The Panopticon*. There was a whole subset of our users who were on the platform to surveil the elite.

Wait, @Gili posted. **Has anyone seen this?** She shared a link to a news article with a photo of Evan wearing a white T-shirt that said "Control the Guns" on the left and "Not Women's Bodies" on the right, his arm around grinning bare-shouldered Devin, at the Richual launch party in October 2016.

I took that photo for the About Us page.

Former *Bachelorette* Contestant Evan Wiley Accused of Inappropriate Conduct by Three Women in Bizarre Fairy Tale Sex Scandal

Entrepreneur, angel investor, self-described feminist, and former *Bachelorette* contestant Evan Wiley has been accused of inappropriate sexual conduct by three women. Fans will remember Wiley as the bachelor who made it to the fantasy suite episode in the Kimberly Hartsong season, shocking viewers by asking Kimberly the question, "What turns you on?" to which she responded, "No one's ever asked me that before."

Wiley was a fan favorite to win Hartsong's heart, but he got into an aggressive confrontation with contestant Brad Bellingham III at the cocktail party just before the rose ceremony, the two trading jabs about who respected women more, until Wiley left the cabana in protest, ranted on camera about the show's culture of "toxic masculinity," and then rode off into the night on a motorbike belonging to hotel staff at Playa Escondida.

For the first time, Hartsong is coming out about what really happened in the fantasy suite. In a post on the website Richual, a social network for women interested in "self-care," Hartsong writes:

> The fantasy suite is supposed to be a night where two people can be intimate with each other. Evan was very gentle. He always asked me what I wanted or what I liked, even though we weren't actually doing anything. It was getting later and later. The camera guys were gone. I was getting tired and I kind of wanted him to take the lead more, to feel wanted, I guess. Finally I must have gotten in bed because it was time to go to sleep and that's when he started. I felt weakened. He said you don't have to do anything, just lie there. I felt tricked when he left the show. Your mind is always going to be like, Was it me? Did I do something wrong?

Wiley is on the board of Richual and the highest equity stakeholder in the company, aside from the cofounders, Devin Avery and Maren Gelb.

One of Wiley's ex-girlfriends, who has asked to remain anonymous, describes Wiley's sexual preferences more explicitly: he prefers sex with women who are "near unconscious."

"At first, it was like a game," she says. "He called it Sleeping Beauty. He asked me to wear a blond wig he had and pretend to be asleep until he, you know, penetrated me. And then I was supposed to wake up."

But Wiley's game turned sinister.

"We went away to this house he had in the country," the woman said. "It was in the spring and I had bad hay fever. I know my sneezing was ruining what was supposed to be this, like, romantic weekend, and he gave me something for my allergies. The next thing I remember, I'm in this dark kind of basement, wearing just a tank top. I went through a couple doors, looking for the bathroom, and when I peed there was blood. Then Evan opened the door, standing there, like, 'You were so hot last night.' We still had another whole day together, and we went to the farmers market and he got me a bouquet of daffodils."

The woman says she never reported the alleged assault to authorities, and stopped responding to his text messages shortly after the weekend, even though he had promised to get her an interview at Richual.

Another woman, Rachelle Tanaka, says she met Evan at a mixer for female entrepreneurs and angel investors around Halloween in 2015. The mixer was a costume party, and Tanaka was dressed as Snow White.

"My company is using VR to disrupt the fitness industry and Evan seemed really interested," Tanaka says. "He was like, 'My place is nearby. Can you show me a demo?' And I said, I can show you a demo right now . . . I had a Google Cardboard viewer in my purse. But he said he couldn't stay much longer, and so I went with him."

Tanaka says that Wiley asked her how much funding she was trying to raise, and when she told him the number, he said, "The number one thing that holds women back is their own limiting beliefs." He suggested she dream bigger.

"Maybe this is naive, but I genuinely thought he was interested in investing in me, in what I was doing," Tanaka says. "He asked really smart questions about the app I was developing and my marketing plan."

They continued to see each other, but Tanaka says that Wiley insisted she wear the costume whenever they had sex. He bought a second costume for her, to keep at his apartment.

"Evan was obsessed with the near-death element of the story and asked if I would give consent to him taking photos of his hands around my neck. I said absolutely not. And he said, I respect that."

Tanaka says she's speaking out publicly to warn other entrepreneurs.

Through his lawyer, Wiley has declined to comment on the story at this time.

NevisFong
@Gili this is just what I was talking about. No content warning before you shared this?

Gili
@NevisFong So sorry!!!

JustDiana
@NevisFong Added to the Google Doc!

Allison
Sounds like my last two boyfriends. Classic narcissistic personality disorder. It's all about power.

NicoletteLee
@Allison I dated NPD too. "A game." BOI BAI

The_s_is_silent
I watched that season of the Bachelorette. The way she kept going back over what happened in her mind . . .
oooooooooof

Aja_dontgothere
IMO, this story is going to get a lot of attention because Evan is a celebrity and now Kimberly Hartsong (is that her name for real?) is a celebrity, but what about WOC who are disproportionally impacted by intimate partner violence? Who's writing about their stories? Why are we always centering white victims?

Gili
@Aja_dontgothere Tanaka is a WOC

Aja_dontgothere
@Gili I didn't say she wasn't?

Felice
@KhadijahWalker how closely do you work with Evan?

NicoletteLee
@Felice @KhadijahWalker wait does he have access to this group???

JustDiana
@Felice @NicoletteLee I will definitely check!

I texted Maren: Please call me when you get this.
Then I emailed Devin:

I'm on my way in.

How Being Investigated by the Secret Service Changed My Life

BY MAREN GELB

Sponsored By Lunar Milk

There's something I've never told anyone before. I have a secret to admit. I have a confession to make. I was investigated by the Secret Service. It's not what you think. It's different than you imagine it would be. It could happen to you.

Are you a woman who believes in something? Not God or your star chart—I mean democracy. Do you understand how at risk we are of losing it? Do you want to call Putin daddy? Do I sound hysterical? Is it because I have a uterus? Do you believe no one should be putting his hands anywhere near your pussy without your consent? Do you believe that if he were your dad, you would definitely distance yourself from him publicly and professionally, atone for the sins of your privilege, and purge yourself of your con artist DNA, not ride the nepotism cabriolet all the way to the White House?

Do you believe Americans have the right to speak truth to power on social media?

I do.

There were two of them. They looked like college admissions officers. The man was wearing a dark suit with a light blue shirt and a striped tie. The woman was in a gray pantsuit and a light pink blouse with the collar unbuttoned. Her hair was limp with blond highlights, tucked behind her ears. Small pearl earrings.

If you think all Secret Service agents wear dark sunglasses, you're totally right, but they take them off inside because they're "just like us."

"Ms. Gelb," the woman said, and shook my hand. "I'm Agent Hannigan and this is Agent Bower."

Sure, they were going to have the female agent speak to me first, to form some kind of phony camaraderie, like I would better comprehend her lady speak.

I could play their game. I was fluent in lady speak, too.

"Can I offer you something to drink, Agent Hannigan?" I said. "Some pinot grigio or a sprinkle of Lunar Milk® in a mug of warm almond milk?"

"What is Lunar Milk®?"

"An adaptogenic super-herb compound."

"What does *adaptogenic* mean?"

"Adaptogens are plant-derived substances used in herbal medicine that increase the body's natural resistance to stress.* Have you been under a lot of stress lately, Agent Hannigan?" Can you even imagine how many house calls like this they had to make? It must be a 24/7 job, checking on Reddit randos. And all I did was tweet a joke. It wasn't even about the president.

"A glass of water would be fine, thanks."

Her partner had a bottle of XXX-flavored Vitamin Water Zero with him already, and I almost asked him to read the ingredients aloud to see if he could pronounce them all, but that seemed needlessly cruel. "John has been a big help, while you were out of town," he said.

My boyfriend, John, is a Democratic Socialist. He was in the bedroom on his laptop, writing a memoir by an heiress to an interstate natural gas pipeline conglomerate fortune, whose philanthropic work funded a network of moderately impactful inner-city charter schools.

"Ms. Gelb, John shared with us an email you sent him on Thursday, February 23, that said, 'Uh oh,' and it linked to your own tweet—"

My socialist sweetheart must have given them my email password.

"Thanks, John," I yelled toward the bedroom. "Thanks for all your help!" I poured myself a generous glass of pinot grigio and sprinkled some Lunar Milk® on top.

"Were you aware, Ms. Gelb, that it's a felony to knowingly and willfully make any threat against the life of the president, or any of his successors, in writing?" Bower asked.

"I'm sorry," I said. "Is Ivanka a 'successor' to the presidency now? Has the United States of America become an aristocracy?"

"I'm just asking the question," he said.

"And I'm just standing up for my right to freedom of speech."

"John tells us you are currently under the care of a mental health professional," Hannigan said.

"I'm on 150 milligrams of Zoloft," I said. "Should I have a lawyer present?"

She recorded something in a notebook. I nursed my wine.

"I know what you're thinking. I shouldn't threaten violence against any woman, not if I'm a feminist, but, to quote Malcolm X: 'We are nonviolent with people who are nonviolent with us.'"

"Freedom of speech actually does not include the right to incite violence," Bower said.

The adaptogens must have been working; my brain fizzed with an alert focus.

Finally I understood what they wanted. They wanted me to say I was sorry.

I started singing "The Star-Spangled Banner" in my head until my eyes filled with tears. "I love my country," I said. "I'm actually from Wisconsin.

"I'm really sorry," I continued. "Yes, I have clinical depression, but no, I don't have violent thoughts or intentions. I'm an ignorant millennial and I apologize. We think we know everything, but we don't. I thought everyone would know I was just joking about the factory fire, but I see now that I didn't read the room."

"What is it that you do for a living, Ms. Gelb?" Bower asked.

"I'm the COO of Richual, a pioneer in the wellness space. We use social technology to connect, cure, and catalyze women to be global changemakers through the simple act of self-care."

They blinked at me.

"I work on making the internet a safer place for women," I said.

Being under investigation by the Secret Service changed my life because for the first time I was on the front lines of understanding how much the elite is invested in stifling women's voices. I will play their game if it allows me to continue my work, but I will not be silent when I see an abuse of power.

These statements have not been evaluated by the Food and Drug Administration. This product is not intended to diagnose, treat, cure, or prevent any disease.

Khadijah

There was no time to shower. I changed out of my yoga pants into jeggings and hustled to the Q, a banana in one hand and my phone in the other. In full-on damage-control mode, Katelyn had emailed the whole team, forbidding anyone from responding to questions about Evan or the article, from the press or from our own users. She added:

> Devin and I are working on a statement. Maren and Khadijah are on their way in.

On the subway nobody gave up their seat for me or even looked at my face. I watched a biracial couple leaning against the doors as they kissed and sipped coffee from paper cups, kissed and sipped, kiss, kiss, kiss. Their public joy seemed uncalled for. Why couldn't they at least pretend to be as miserable as the rest of us? I was sweating through my blouse, holding my coat in my arms like a puffy barricade.

Come back. I forget what you look like , I texted Adam.

Soon , he said. How are you feeling?

Drama at work , I typed, debating whether or not he needed all the details. His interest in following the daily play-by-play of the internet was about as great as my interest in learning the entire catalog of Phish. Whenever I talked about work Adam never remembered who was who. "Devin is the investor or Evan is the investor?"

"Devin is the CEO."

"Which is the one who calls you K. in emails?"

"That's Evan."

I wanted Adam's sympathy, but not his concern. Had to skip yoga , I said. I made a frowny face with a colon and a parenthesis, the only way to communicate my disappointment in a language his ancient cell phone would understand.

Evan had once stopped to ask if my hair was "real" during a board meeting when I was there to take notes for Maren. After streaming the ESPN doc on O.J., he was curious whether or not I believed O.J. should have been acquitted. "I was five years old during the trial," I told him. Evan had also personally nominated me for *Forbes*'s 30 Under 30 list and taken me to dinner at Dirt Candy to ask what my long-term career goals were. He had never once made a pass at me.

"Is It Because I'm Black? One Woman Speaks Up About Not Being Targeted for Sexual Abuse in Her White Workplace," I mused. I remembered all the essays I'd read online by women who'd never been catcalled, "not even by construction workers," and how that was its own form of marginalization, not being beautiful enough to be objectified.

There was an upside to all of this. There were five board members and three of them were male investors. If Evan was ousted and a woman took his seat, Maren would have the leverage to institute a paid family leave policy across the board, even for hourly community moderators. We could give health benefits to our part-timers. I could persuade Devin that the installation of a chill lactation oasis onsite would pay for itself in positive press.

I waited at my desk to be needed. I was too distracted to do anything but play with my lavender-scented therapeutic meditation putty and check the CMS to be sure the scheduled posts met Maren's standard of two stock photos with women of color for every one stock photo of all white women:

**Are You Eating Too
Much Before Your Reformer Class?**

**Ancient Fasting Wisdom That Will Blow
Your Mind (And Clear Your Gut)**

The Real Reason You Think You Need a Snack

**Can't Stop Thinking About Food? How to Stop
Obsessive Thoughts When You're Cleansing**

**Five Sex Toys That Will Make You
Literally Give Up on Human Intimacy**

**If You Aren't Doing Kegels at Your Desk
Right Now, You're Not Doing Enough**

Squish squish squish.

I Slacked Diana and asked her to help me with a project in the beauty closet, the only place in the office with nontransparent walls and a door. The floor-to-ceiling storage shelves were stocked with samples of foundation in every shade of milk, cheek tint to raise skin cancer awareness, cheek tint that changed color based on your mood, cheek tint with a built-in mace spritzer, boxes of lucid dreaming tea, a Winona Ryder and Johnny Depp–themed tarot deck, individually wrapped sheet masks that said "Charcoal Power" below a drawing of a black fist, bottles of SPF 50 hairspray, blue vials of hyaluronic acid, and tiny brown jars of ashwagandha powder.

"I know her," Diana said.

"Know who?"

"The ex-girlfriend in the article. Do you think I should text her? Tell her that I work at Richual?"

Diana seemed thrilled to be so close to the eye of the shitstorm. She wanted to be acknowledged as an essential player in the drama.

"Let's focus," I said. "I want you to go on Slack and tell them that we'll share more information on Evan as soon as we have it."

"Which Slack? The internal Slack?"

"No, the *Stay Woke, Y'All* Slack." Saying the words out loud was more humiliating than seeing them on a screen. The title had to go.

"Got it," Diana said.

"Pretend you don't know anything because, um, you *don't*

know anything. Get them back on topic. I need examples of influencers who generate good conversation. Ask them—"

Maren was calling me. I texted back: Meet me in beauty closet.

"Ask them to share the last post that made them mad, okay?"

"Fo sho," Diana said.

"Oh hey." Maren squeezed in. Her greasy hair was piled in a nest on top of her head. One brown strand hung down in back. There were purple moons under her eyes.

"You were just at Evan's house, right?" Diana said.

"There's a post I just added to the queue. Can you add the sponsor logo? But don't publish it yet."

"You mean right now?"

"Unless Khadijah has you working on something else."

"Go," I told Diana. "I'll catch up with you later."

The air was stale and claustrophobic. A bead of sweat ran down my low back. I had to pee but willed myself to hold it. As much as my body expanded in space, I reminded myself of the ways in which I remained its master.

"I'd love it if you could look at my post, too," Maren said. "It's almost like a manifesto of my value system. I haven't written anything that long since college. I don't know how you do it three times a day!" *Eight times a day*, I wanted to correct her but didn't. "But I think if we don't speak up with our voices, who will? It's like that poem, 'First they came for the Jews, and I didn't know what to say . . . '" She continued rambling as she took out her phone to look it up.

I had no idea when I would have another minute alone in a room with her.

"No, it's 'First they came for the socialists, and I did not speak out, because I was not a socialist.' Isn't wifi incredible? Too often we take it for granted. You can look up Nazi stuff whenever you want, check your email, read the—"

"Maren, listen," I said. "There's something I have to tell you. I'm sorry to be telling you like this." *Don't apologize*, I thought. *The script. The script. Stick to the script.*

"Your face looks different," Maren said, squinting. "Did you get your brows waxed?"

"It's not that."

"Don't tell me," she said. "I already know."

"You do?"

"Devin texted me the article. And she doesn't even know." Maren was pulling on one eyelid and blinking.

"Doesn't even know what?" *You always put Maren and her feelings first. She's a grown-up. She can handle it.*

"Is there something in my eye?"

"I don't think so."

"There's an eyelash or something. I can't get it."

Just say, "I'm pregnant." Say, "Maternity leave."

My phone buzzed. It was Devin: Do you know where Maren is? I lost her.

"We have to go meet Devin," I said, letting myself off the hook. There would be another opportunity. This was not it.

"When's the last time you ate something?" I asked her. I grabbed a bottle of aloe vera water from the shelf and two packs of organic multivitamin gummies, the closest thing there was in the closet to actual food.

...

Devin was facedown on the massage chair while Sharona, our South African in-house masseuse, dug the ball of an elbow into her left trapezius. Katelyn sat at Devin's desk, as engrossed in her laptop as if she were Rami Malek hacking a bank.

"Read it again," Devin said.

"Richual supports—no, Richual *stands behind* board member . . ."

"I'm not cosigning that," Maren said.

"It's not a contract," Devin said. "It's a statement."

"Let me write it then."

"You can't do everything, Maren!"

"Mommy and Daddy are fighting," Katelyn muttered to herself, without taking her eyes off the screen.

"We're not fighting," Maren said. "I just don't think we should give Evan a 'get out of jail free' card. How does that look for our brand? Self-care for all victims except, like, the ones whose abuser we know personally?"

"Harder," Devin said to Sharona. "What about Ivanka? Was she not the victim of your tweet? Did you ever think about her feelings? She's a mom of three!"

"Did you wear your MAGA hat when you went to the polls, Devin?"

Maren sounded like one of the women on Slack. Having an audience only made her meaner. No one had the power to make her apologize.

Devin said nothing.

"I think," I said, "that maybe one of the positive takeaways from this is that the tweet wasn't all bad, because we got ten thousand new users from it. Because being angry takes a toll on your mental health. And Richual offers an antidote to that."

"Khadijah gets me," Maren said, shooting a pack of gummies into her mouth.

"What I'm hearing from everyone," Katelyn said, "is that we need to control the message about Evan and get ahead of the narrative."

Too late, I thought. In the background, without me, the conversation continued on Slack, on Twitter, on Richual itself. The virus was already spreading.

"Evan should apologize," Maren said. "That's how we spin it. Evan should be the one worrying about the wording of *his* statement. He can defend himself. Or whatever. He can use Katelyn if he wants to."

"Borrow Katelyn," I suggested.

"What?"

"You said 'use,' but I think you meant 'borrow.'"

"Stop," Devin said to Sharona, holding up an arm as pale as a wishbone. When she lifted her head from the face rest, her cheeks were damp and splotchy. "Maren, these women are *lying*."

"How do you know?"

"Why are they saying this now? Evan is helping us raise our series B and they come out with this *now*?"

"You think this story about Evan is going to keep us from closing the round?" I asked.

"Fuck," Maren said, rubbing her eye again. "But that's insane. That's . . . victim blaming."

"Is it?" Katelyn asked. "I'll google it."

"Devin is blaming the victims for not coming forward sooner."

"No," Devin said, standing up. She looked Maren in the eye. "You're not listening to me. I'm blaming them for making up that they're victims in the first place. Evan didn't do anything with them that they didn't want to do."

"What are you—a sex psychic?" Maren asked.

Sharona looked at me and gestured to the massage chair, my only shot at escape. I shook my head.

"If someone accused you of abusing them, I would defend you," Devin said. "Because that's how much I care about you."

"I can't imagine a scenario in which I would abuse someone."

"Exactly."

"Has anyone spoken to Evan?" I asked.

Katelyn shook her head at me.

"I already know my opinion," Devin said. "My opinion about Evan is that he's innocent. As a woman, am I allowed to have an opinion, or . . . ?"

Maren took her hair down, twisted it, pinned it back up, and straddled the massage chair. "This is about our company values. *Women are people. All people are human beings. Believe women.* Those first three commandments are what we stand for. It's bigger than you, Devin. It's bigger than any of us."

"I also want to know why," Devin said, "Kimberly Hartsong is posting the name of her abuser"—*abuser* in air quotes—"on Richual. Is that not explicit in the FAQ that *you* made, Maren? About how to write powerful confessional content? No names?"

"I had nothing to do with Kimberly's post," Maren said. "I have not interacted with her once."

"I think you at least owe me an apology about the MAGA comment." Her cheeks burned pink.

"You're right," Maren said. "I'm sorry. You would never be seen in something so ugly."

"I'm confident there's a way to balance our support of Evan and our female empowerment messaging," Katelyn said. "I'll have another draft in a sec."

"I'm sorry," I said, "but I really have to pee."

"Are you drinking too much water?" Devin called after me. "Drinking too much water is dangerous!"

FOR IMMEDIATE RELEASE

March 1, 2017

~~RICHUAL STANDS BEHIND BOARD MEMBER EVAN WILEY~~

~~INNOCENT UNTIL PROVEN GUILTY: QUESTIONS REMAIN ABOUT SEXUAL ASSAULT ALLEGATIONS AGAINST FEMINIST ALLY EVAN WILEY~~

HAPPY WOMEN'S HISTORY MONTH FROM ALL OF US AT RICHUAL

Whether you're ~~booking a spa day~~ scheduling a session with your energy worker, sharing a cold bottle (or two) of Cava with your besties, or committing to a thirty-day gut-balancing reset in the Richual app (#YouGotThis), Women's History Month is the perfect time to honor the strength and courage of the amazing women who've come before us by taking care of our whole selves so we have the energy to *make* history.

Here at Richual, we're making history by employing a diverse staff of 100 percent women who are 100 percent themselves every day.

~~"It's unfortunate when women believe the only power they have is in taking successful women down," CEO Devin Avery remarks. "That these allegations would come to light when we're on the verge of closing on our Series B is . . . I have to raise an eyebrow at that."~~

Together, we're supporting women by building a digital product ~~that supports~~ that shows that you're not alone in trying ~~to live your best life~~ to find optimum balance in your career, relationships, and well-being.

"It has been one of the great privileges of my career to see how Richual has lifted up so many women's voices," COO Maren Gelb says. "All over the world, women have been through so many painful experiences and to be able to create a community where the stories of those experiences can be shared is a tremendous opportunity and also a responsibility I take very seriously."

Regarding the ~~sexual~~ behavioral misconduct allegations against Evan Wiley, a Richual board member and longtime feminist ally, CEO Devin Avery says, "At Richual, we believe women. We also know that, sadly, a small percentage of these kinds of allegations are falsely reported and sadly, this is one of those tiny percentages. It is a shame that these are not real victims, but I pray that this unfortunate circumstance will not silence the true victims of abusive men that are still out there."

In honor of #WomensHistoryMonth, check out our slideshow of the pioneering women who have changed health history in the United States, from Jane Fonda ~~to Margaret Sanger~~ to Michelle Obama to Lulu Hunt Peters, who taught America calorie counting in 1918. #Legend

Devin

I left the office at 5:00 so I could grab a thirty-five-minute Heart: Gratitude session at my meditation studio. I brought my attention to my breath. I brought my attention to my breath. I brought my attention to my breath. Who was the ex in the article, the girl who wanted a job at Richual? I hoped it wasn't our intern Chloé. How fucked up would that be? Me and her and Evan were all just in the conference room together for the pitch meeting. I replayed the sight of her body, as she raised one hand in the air, the good student. *Notice when your mind wants to wander from the sensation of the air passing through your nostrils*, said the voice on the wireless headphones. We were all wearing wireless headphones. Evan didn't need any of them. Evan had me. What more did he want, what did I not have enough of, how much more on-demand could I be? I brought my attention to my breath. Grateful for my legs, my lungs, my 64 bpm resting heart rate. Grateful to not have to work in indentured nail salon servitude.

Grateful to be able to afford my recurring monthly subscriptions. Grateful for Evan. Grateful for Richual.

"How was it?" the mindfulness attendant asked when we returned our headphones.

"I feel so much better," I told her. You always had to be gracious with these people, in case they recognized you. One misstep and the eyewitness testimony would be all over social media, blunt force trauma to your influence.

I walked the six blocks to Pheel and changed into my black Adidas by Stella McCartney warp-knit yoga tights and white "Here to Create" T-shirt. I put my mat down in the sanctuary. But Tressa wasn't there. Tressa was always there on Wednesdays. Where was Tressa?

"Excuse me?" I said to the woman wearing a headset standing near a pedestal of potted orchids. "I'm looking for Tressa's class."

"I'm her sub Jen," she said. *Jen?* Jen's frizzy ponytail and faded athletic wear made her look like a Zumba instructor at Crunch. No way was she certified in the Pheel methodology.

"Jen, did something happen to Tressa? I know she's had surgery before?" I realized that in all the years I'd known Tressa, I'd never asked for her number. We'd never gotten chai. I felt so close to her and what did she know about me? My life?

"She had tickets to *Hamilton*," Jen said.

I retrieved my phone from my locker and set it near my mat. "I might have an emergency and have to leave," I told Jen as she dimmed the lights. Many of the regulars hadn't shown up. Maybe they checked the website and saw the sub. I hadn't checked the website. I had trusted Tressa would be here.

Babe, are you okay? I texted Evan. If you don't feel like talking, that's okay. I set the phone to vibrate with his response.

Jen's playlist was basic. I didn't know anything about her story or what she'd overcome. It was just four minutes of alternating pistol squats with no purpose or meaning behind them. "Let the feeling show you how strong you are," she said. *O rly?*

The last thing I would ever want to do is hurt someone, Evan texted. I had Kimberly Hartsong's enthusiastic consent but you wouldn't know that from what she said on Richual. It's so isolating. No one cares what I have to say.

I do, I wrote back, in plank pose, making a game of it, holding it even after Jen said we were done.

Sometimes I fantasized about quitting Richual. *I know this amazing team will continue its mission of healing work without me!* I would write in my goodbye post. I would have been with Evan if I could. It wasn't as though I needed the salary. The company was standing between us and what our relationship could be if we had more time to work on it. I could rehabilitate his image in the press. We could volunteer to plant an organic vegetable garden with students in Harlem. We could sit next to each other at a silent vipassana retreat in Myanmar, eating oatmeal without speaking, watching our thoughts come and go without speaking, having sex without speaking. I pictured us in black tie at a gala to raise money to treat obstetric fistulas in Africa. There was so much more you could do if you didn't have to work. I never told Maren how much I hated working because I knew she would say that was unfeminist and it was super important to her that I be a feminist with her.

I was twenty-nine years old and I'd never really had a boy-friend. I dated men who begged me to eat a bacon cheeseburger so they could watch, who wanted to give me a good dicking while I alternated between three-legged dog pose and plow pose and happy baby pose like I was an ensemble member of Cirque du Soleil, who told me to just "relax" and have a beer even after I told them I was gluten free. All the work I put into my body—who was it even for? For guys who got off on the idea of fitting some-thing big inside something small? It wasn't for other women. They didn't like me. Pictures of my face and body stood in for everything they hated about privileged white women whose lives were *so easy*.

The way that Evan touched me, stroked me, licked me, looked at me, denied me, tied me up, made the rules, made me wait, made me think *This is what my body is for.* I couldn't imagine ever meeting anyone else I'd have the same chemistry with. I didn't understand why Evan even needed to go after these other women who didn't want to submit the way I did.

...

At the Halloween party in 2015, Maren went as Furiosa, and in her boots, my head only came up to her boobs. I was Margot Tenenbaum, but I got too hot in my mink coat from the RealReal and had to drape it over an ottoman and then no one recognized who I was, even with the red barrette and the perfect raccoon eyes. "Lolita?" someone guessed. I gestured with my unlit ciga-rette. "Gwyneth Paltrow?" someone dressed like a judge with a frilly neck ruffle said and I said yes, and we talked about an article I'd read that said G.P. smoked one cigarette a week and whether or not that was a better form of balance than total abstinence because at least you're not depriving yourself.

The mixer was at a WeWork on Park Avenue South, in a common space adorned with crystal chandeliers. The ginormous gourmet cheese platters from Murray's on the coffee tables remained mostly untouched.

"We should separate," Maren said, folding an entire sheet of prosciutto into her mouth. "And network." She wanted us to try out our idea—a time management app that would help you find more minutes in your day for self-care and schedule it—on other female entrepreneurs, the busiest people of all.

I asked for a glass of sauv blanc with a splash of sparkling water from the bartender and tried the pitch I'd practiced with Maren on a girl in a sexy tampon costume. "And our revenue would come from partnering with barre studios or Drybar or spin studios or those salons where the fish eat the dead skin on your feet, like as a referral fee, for users booking directly through the app." I couldn't tell if she was really listening to me because she was trying to adjust the cup padding in her white leotard.

"Have you considered gamifying?"

"What do you mean?"

"Like you get points for how much you do to take care of yourself and you can compete with your friends!"

"Would you use that?"

"You can tell this is blood, right?" She was wearing a pair of red boy shorts on top of the leotard, and red tights.

"Yeah, it's super cute," I said. "So if we made a game where you and your friends tried to see who was the best at taking care of themselves, that's something you would play?"

"That's not exactly what I meant," the tampon said. "Excuse me, but I have to go say hi to this person I haven't seen in forever!"

I felt like I had messed something up—I should have asked what she was working on first and then shown active listening by saying *mmm* and repeating back what she said, before I started talking about myself. I needed to find the ladies' room so I could do some mindfulness exercises in private, but then I noticed Snow White sitting down at the edge of the ottoman where I'd left my coat, running her hands up and down, and mouthing *It's real* to a friend dressed as a pumpkin spice latte with "Britni" written across her midriff. Then Snow White reclined all the way, treating my mink like a bedspread on *Game of Thrones*. I felt hot all over again, and the place in my brain where I should have been able to find the words to ask her to stop doing that, please, was empty. It reminded me of high school, when I'd walked into English class to find a new transfer student sitting in my desk and instead of saying something, I spent the rest of the year sitting in the back of the room with the drug addicts, who convinced the teacher to take us on a field trip to a local mental hospital where famous poets were once detained. I needed to find a bathroom.

"Is that Margot Tenenbaum?"

At first I didn't recognize him. I hadn't seen Evan in three years and he had more facial hair now.

"Oh my god, hi!" I said and gave him a hug. He held onto me a little longer than I expected and we were so close that I could

smell the lemony bergamot and salty sea spray of his Acqua Di
Gio cologne.

"Hey, I'm sorry about your dad," Evan said.

"It's okay," I said. I put the cigarette to my lips, forgetting it was
unlit. Felt like an idiot. Rolled my eyes at myself so he would know
I felt like an idiot. Replayed the hug my arms still remembered.

"No, I should have been there at the funeral. I'm sorry. I went
down to Nicaragua for an immersive language program and
ended up staying to redesign their website and set up their social
accounts and teach them how to target Facebook ads to assholes
like me. *Lo siento.*"

Evan plucked a purple grape from the stem on his plate and
held it in the air for my mouth to meet. It was like we'd climbed
back inside the skin of our former selves, how easily we fit together. I remembered meeting him for the first time sophomore
year, when I was hooking up with his brother Zack and we went
to a party at Delta Sig, where Evan was VP.

"Do you remember that day we went to Morningside Park and
Zack was so hungover that he—"

"Oh, that's funny, I wondered who had the most convincing
man costume." Maren was back. Whenever we were around guys,
she made jokes that were 10 percent too aggressive. Her own boyfriend was one of her victims.

But Evan took it in stride. "I know, I goofed. I think my assistant meant to put this girl power meetup on her calendar, but she
put it on mine. Maybe she's on my conference call tonight with
these guys who say they've got the next Dogecoin. Hope she's
taking good notes. Evan Wiley." He stuck out his hand.

"Evan and Devin," Maren said. "Cute." I could hear the air quotes in her voice.

"This is my business partner, Maren," I added. "Maren, Evan and I went to college together. He's an *angel investor* now."

"Well, in that case, I love your costume," Maren said.

"To *Mad Max*," Evan said, raising his bottle of Stella.

"To Furiosa," Maren said. They clinked.

...

Dad always made sure to text or call me when he traveled for work, especially after Mom died. I always knew what time zone he was in. He sent photos of giant electric trees at night in Singapore, a cat café in Tokyo, sunrises and sunsets snapped from his window seat above the clouds. He died in his Hong Kong hotel room on a Saturday. I should have been worried on Sunday when I didn't hear from him, but I was running errands all day. I spent an hour at Barney's trying to decide whether to buy a studded black leather skirt off the sale rack that was one size too small. I couldn't latch the hook above the back zipper and I should have put it back on the rack, but instead I turned it into a goal. My father was dead of a heart attack and I was standing in a room with mirrors on three sides literally gazing at my navel. I bought the skirt but never took the tags off. I got the call at 9:51 p.m. It was Monday morning in Hong Kong.

I called my aunt in Rye and I don't even remember what we said to each other. We just cried and I heard her telling her husband and he said, "What? What?" and she yelled, *"Michael is dead!*" And I lied and said I was going to bed just to not have to listen to that anymore and she said, "Sweet dreams, sweetheart."

Each day that passed seemed longer than the day that had preceded it. An hour wasn't sixty minutes; it was ninety. By the time I fell asleep, it was sunrise. My eyes were bloodshot, a horror show. When Mom died, I don't remember the nature of time changing. Her cancer meant months of anticipation. The final weeks of hospice care at home were further preparation. I think I kept waiting for her to like me, to have some kind of last-minute revelation about what it meant to have me for a daughter, but the closest we ever got was when she asked me to apply her Advanced Night Repair serum to her face and neck. She did it. She won the battle against aging—dead at fifty-seven. There were Facebook tributes to her obvious beauty and philanthropic work, women coming over, bringing prepared food from Citarella we just had to reheat. A few of my college friends came to the funeral to offer their condolences:

"Your mom was so pretty."

"You look just like her."

For a little while, it was like my childhood fantasy fulfilled: having my dad all to myself, not having to share him with someone who needed so much care and attention. But Dad wasn't on the school fundraising committee; he didn't sit on the board of my mom's foundation that gave grants to arts organizations. He never joined Facebook. I had no one to mourn with. Beyond me, his life was his work. His office delivered a bouquet of lilies and a tower of chocolates.

I posted four photos to Instagram of me as a little girl so blond my hair was almost white and my dad with his early nineties 'stache and said, **Still in shock. Can't believe he's gone.** Every few minutes, I checked my notifications, comparing the number of likes to the number of followers I had. The numbers were way off. Why wasn't anyone ringing my doorbell? Or at least texting me to see if I was okay? Had I not struck the appropriate balance between cute and destroyed? Also, how was it possible that every single person I followed was getting married that weekend but had not invited me? I scanned the bodies of the brides for extra fat where their upper arm squeezed the side of their chest. I cried at every picture of a father of the bride.

Leslie Royce, a lawyer who had known my dad and who had once helped me with a contract thing for my coaching business, texted me, Oh my God! Michael was the best. Call me anytime. I'm here for you. Whatever you need help with. To be polite, I told her thank you and that I was fine. My aunt texted me questions about returning the remains and I said, I have literally no clue. Whatever you want to do. I'm going to take a nap. ♥ I drank coconut water. I ate an entire package of Twizzlers. I texted my therapist: My dad died. Can you talk? I saw the three dots appear like she was typing her response, but then they went away. I ordered a chicken burrito bowl with extra sour cream and an orange Jarritos on Seamless. I made a list of who my bridesmaids would be and couldn't think of one. I drank more coconut water and puked until I saw the base layer of Twizzlers come up. Relieved, I cleaned up with a Clorox toilet wand and took a long shower.

I was shaving my legs, carefully navigating around the eczema patches, when a thought came to me that had never come to me

before. The hand holding the razor seemed to be in conversation
with a part of my mind that I wished would shut the fuck up.
Who would find me if I did something? No one. *Would that be a good
thing?* The hot water hit my back like tiny needles. My mouth
tasted like smoky bile from the chicken. I sucked up some phlegm
at the back of my throat and spit three times, *ptuh ptuh ptuh*, like
I was creating a barrier between myself and evil. Then I pulled
the curtain aside and threw the razor across the bathroom.

There was a text from Maren when I got out: Holy shit are you
okay?

We hadn't known each other for very long. It was light outside
when I called her, but I couldn't tell whether it was 8:00 a.m. or
8:00 p.m.

"I'm an orphan," I said. "I'm a twenty-seven-year-old orphan."

"That's crazy."

"When my friend Daphne's stepdad died, I sent her flowers
and she can't even comment on my posts?"

"Maybe she's sending you flowers right now."

"She doesn't know my address."

"Are you sure?"

"She doesn't have my new address."

There was an awkward pause I rushed to fill.

"When I was in the shower, I kind of thought of hurting myself," I said. Now I was crying quietly, covering my mouth so she
wouldn't hear.

"Jesus, let's call someone," Maren said. "Who could we call?
Like a best friend. A cousin? I don't think you should be alone
right now. You can share the contact with me and I can call for

you," she rattled on. The more I tried not to cry, the more my chest pumped like a machine.

"Do you think maybe you could come over?" I asked.

"Sure," Maren said, sounding surprised. "Of course I can."

"I'll give you my address."

"I have your address. I sent you a postcard from my vacation, remember?"

She slept all night in my bed.

...

"I met Maren right before my dad died," I was telling Evan at the mixer. "And the two of us, we just realized how hard it is for women to take care of themselves sometimes and we thought about what we could create to make self-care more—"

"More of a given, less of a luxury," Maren said.

"Yes, and but still with that luxury feeling," I added. Maren was the one who taught me *yes and*.

"Luxury," Evan said. "I dig it. My girlfriend—well, I guess she's my ex-girlfriend now—got me into Kiehl's beard grooming oil and now . . ."

"Now it's your ritual," I said, zooming in on the word *ex*.

Maren grabbed my shoulders and I was so startled, I dropped my cigarette. "That's it!" she said. "Sorry, I didn't mean to scare you. But that's it; that's the name." She grabbed her phone from her tote bag and opened her notes app. "R-I-C-H-U-A-L, get it?"

I'd never seen Maren look so happy about anything before. I

wrapped my arms around her waist, which was cinched with five different leather belts, and smiled at Evan while he took our picture.

"The founders," he said. "I'll tag you."

"Wait," I said, "can I see it before you post?"

"I'm searching right now to see if I can buy the domain," Maren said.

Snow White was walking in my direction, smiling. Maybe she recognized my costume and now understood the coat was mine. Maybe I wouldn't need to say anything at all.

"Excuse me," she said.

"No worries," I said. "You didn't know."

"Excuse me," she said again, and I realized she wasn't smiling at me at all. She was smiling at Evan.

"Rachelle Tanaka," Snow White said, holding out a hand.

"Hey," Evan said. "Have we met before?"

"No, I just recognized you from your Twitter profile. I'm @TanakaTabata. I think we follow each other?"

"It's available!" Maren said.

"These are my friends," Evan said, "Maren and Devin. They're cofounders of a startup that's empowering women to take the time to add some luxury back into their self-care routines."

"That's incredible," Rachelle said. She was wearing the most beautiful black-green eyelashes. "Have you been following Carlotta Krause-Steubenfeld? She is doing something similar, but with gels."

"Gels?" I asked.

"Oh my god, I can't *believe* you haven't heard of her! Let's exchange info, I'd love to introduce you. I think you're working in a very similar space. Very similar. It's a space where she's really dominating. Carlotta is amazing."

Everyone had their phones out now, so I got mine out, too, and sent an email to Rachelle so she would have my contact info.

"I'm texting her right now," Rachelle said. "What did you say the name was?"

"Richual," Maren said. "Richual, R-I-C-H, dot com. We're doing a redesign right now, so she won't be able to see much yet on the homepage."

I opened my calorie-counter app and entered the four ounces of wine and three grapes. Then I opened Instagram and saw that Evan had already posted the photo and it was from my bad side, where my underbite was worse. It was too late to redo.

"I can't believe this is where we're meeting, of all places," Rachelle said to Evan. "I saw on social that you're into counting macros. Can I steal you for a few minutes to tell you about what I'm working on?"

"Ladies, I'll catch up with you later. Let's get a lunch on the books. Sugarfish?"

"I love Sugarfish," I said, but it was too late. He was already gone.

"Well, that was productive," Maren said. "Should we go eat some real food?"

"I need you to do something for me."

"What?"

"Please will you go get my fur? There's a human tampon sitting on it."

"So tell her to get off."

"*Please*, Furiosa," I said. I thought I might start crying so I laughed instead, so hard I doubled over, shaking.

Maren

My mom and dad never married. It wouldn't even be accurate to say that he left her because they were never really together. I was their John Lennon meme: the life that happened when they were making other plans.

Steve already had a wife. I wanted to know all about this other family (a girl, a boy, another girl just a few months younger than I was) and what they looked like (braces, Little League uniform, freckles) so I could compare myself in the mirror. A couple of times, when we stopped by their house so my mom could pick something up, I saw a pale face watching through the blinds of an upstairs window. By my estimation, they inhabited a castle. Our house could have fit in the garage.

Did the face in the window mean they thought about us as much as I thought about them? I believed the haunting should be mutual.

If I wanted to, I could see my dad every day. All I had to do was turn on Channel 7 before school and there he was, delivering the news. "Wake up with Steve and Stacey, starting at five thirty," the promos said. I inherited his broad forehead, his thick brow, the dismissive expression he gave Stacey if she flubbed one of her lines on the prompter. I was the kid in class who wouldn't hesitate to correct the teacher, even if it got me in trouble. I memorized the date of every field trip, the correct spelling of Principal Szalkowski's name, the rule on tank top strap width. Not the prettiest in school portraits, or the best runner in PE, or the girl you could trust to keep your secrets. I was the know-it-all.

The one thing I didn't know was how much Steve was supposed to be paying in child support, but he paid something. For much of my childhood, my mom and I lived in a small white rental house with two bedrooms and a huge backyard we shared with the family who owned the main house. I was allowed to play on the trampoline if I was invited, but our landlord's kids were older and hardly ever included me in their games.

One winter, the checks stopped. Mom took a second job, waking up at three thirty in the morning to deliver newspapers in the frigid dark, before she got me ready for school. Sometimes she put her head on the kitchen table and passed out cold while I ate my oatmeal.

"Why don't you tell on Daddy?" I asked, shaking her arm.

"Who would I tell?"

There was a call-in part of the morning show, where viewers could dial in and talk to Steve or Stacey about a local issue, like zoning for a new mall or a scandal with the school board. I had watched so many times I knew the number by heart.

"715-777-1515," I sang to her, making a phone with my fingers. "Hello? I'm a longtime resident of Marathon County and I'm calling because one of your employees is a very bad man."

This made her laugh, but not as much as I hoped. She rubbed one eye with a knuckle.

"And I think you should fire him," I continued.

"Don't say that," she said. "Then Steve really wouldn't be able to help us."

You forgive the guy who writes the check. You stay optimistic that it will all sort itself out, while you try to fill in the gaps created by his negligence.

She accepted our landlords' invitation to attend a meeting at their house about a business opportunity to achieve financial independence by working only part time. All we had to do was brush our teeth with Glister toothpaste and start taking Nutrilite vitamins.

"You and me," she said, "we're dreamers."

There were black vinyl organizers filled with cassette tapes of motivational speeches that she listened to in the car to and from work, to and from seminars. *Show the plan, share the dream!* I chanted it with her. Our positive thinking must have worked: the proof was in the visit from a couple in her upline, who drove to our house in their tan RV and I got to go inside for a tour. I thought everything would be miniature, like a dollhouse, but the bed inside was way bigger than my own. I marveled at the way a little table folded down from the interior wall. If this was the house they lived in when they were on the road, what did their real house look like?

Our monthly product order, the tapes, the tickets to seminars and conferences, gas to drive to meetings, the copies of *Rich Dad, Poor Dad* and *How to Win Friends and Influence People*—all went on her new credit cards.

"I'm fired up," she told me.

So was I. That summer, I was allowed to go on the trampoline whenever I wanted.

I still didn't know how much my mom lost, trying to go Diamond.

. . .

Our kitchen smelled like old bananas. There was a coffee-stained Rachel Maddow mug and a small tower of plates stacked in the sink. A take-out container speckled with rice had been left out for at least two days. Was the sheen of grime on the countertops representative of the slob I cohabited with or was it evidence that my beloved was too dedicated to his art to be disturbed by domestic chaos? According to the fridge magnet John got me for my birthday, I should "Keep Calm and Drink Wine."

"I was just about to do those," he called, when I had already started soaping the sponge. I ignored him and scrubbed at the brown ring around the faucet handle and the old scuzz under the dish-drying rack. I pictured Evan at home, lighting a fire by tapping an app, commanding Alexa to play Nina Simone, drinking something expensive in a glass with a single giant ice cube, examining the life choices that had brought him to this moment, the privileges that protected him from being held accountable sooner.

"You can take out the garbage," I told John.

"Not tonight."

"Yes tonight."

"I'll do it first thing tomorrow," he said, planting a kiss on my head. I was trying to scrape some congealed egg off a plate with my thumbnail. It wasn't even my egg. It was his egg. John poured me a glass of pinot grigio.

"Listen to this." John held his phone in front of his face. "This woman on Facebook—her profile picture is an American eagle holding a gun. She posted this under an MSNBC clip: *So what if Jared Kushner met with the Russian ambassador? Hillary didn't win, libtards!*"

"Do you want to get Thai tonight?" I said. "Or Indian."

"So I commented: *Reagan would be rolling over in his grave if he knew how many American conservatives were fans of Putin.*"

"That's what Obama said."

"What?"

"What you just said. Obama said that."

"Maybe," John said, frowning. "Empanadas?"

"I'm sick of empanadas."

"The fancy mac and cheese place?"

When my hands were dry, I found our most recent order and clicked Add to Cart, charged it to my credit card. John hadn't said anything about the money he borrowed and I carried around his debt like my pet, stroking it when I wanted to remind myself how much he owed me.

...

On our first date, John showed me his business card. On one side, there was an outline of a ghost. On the other, the same ghost but with a silhouette of a man inside. I thought this was very clever, possibly because this was the first date I'd been on with someone important enough to have their own business card.

"How much does someone get for ghostwriting a celebrity's book?" I asked him.

"Guess," he said.

"A million dollars."

His cheeks burned red and he shook his head.

"*Two* million dollars?" I hadn't yet learned how to read his expressions.

"No, it's usually a six-figure deal and I get a percentage of that. Some upfront, some later. But I'm, uh, in between projects right now."

"Let me buy the next round," I said and he didn't argue.

John's ex cheated on him for months and he never had a clue. Once she finally told him, he was so depressed he couldn't work. He lived on unemployment and credit cards. I met him while I was working at my nonprofit, so we were broke equals. We went on cheap dates: take-out arepas, dark dive bars with pitchers of bad cold beer, midnight showings of classic movies where we smuggled in our own Raisinets.

We'd only been out a few times when he started telling everyone about me. The breakup with his ex had been so bad, like stage IV cancer, a life-threatening event you don't recover from, and I was his miracle remission. I was his prize for surviving. Like a minor celebrity, I was beloved by people I hadn't even met. When John read his friends' emails and texts aloud to me, I flushed with happiness. One said, after seeing my picture, that we're biologically drawn to people with big eyes, because it makes us want to take care of them. I thought I could take care of myself just fine thank you, but if my eyes made John choose me, then yes, I wanted to be chosen.

Now that John was working again, when he did get a big check, once every six or twelve or eighteen months, we splurged. He didn't have the foresight to take $20,000 and divide it into allocations for the months when there would be no checks at all. I could tell him what to do, but it wasn't my money. I wanted to feel carefree, too. Let's go to Blue Hill at Stone Barns and eat waste-fed pork ribs with pickled lardo and fiddlehead ferns. He needed a new MacBook. I needed *Hamilton* tickets.

This is what it will be like all the time, I told myself, *once Richual is acquired*. It was like a dress rehearsal for my future life. Trying on clothes off the rack without checking the price tags first.

We refilled our Metro cards and paid rent. Then John took whatever was left and sent it to the credit card company, or made a back-taxes payment, and we were back to living on my salary, ordering Seamless, entertaining ourselves with HBO Go.

When I needed a rush of sanctimoniousness, I could always go online and read other people's money diaries. There was a urologist who didn't think she'd ever be able to buy a home because the only time she ever felt good was when she was shopping and all her disposable income went to paying her credit card balances.

An itemized breakdown of the skincare products in her medicine cabinet totaled $3,600. *You're an idiot*, I thought. I religiously followed the blog of a single woman who shared her income and expenses every month as she tried to pay off the debt she'd accumulated having a baby: first, two rounds of IVF not covered by the only insurance plan she could afford as an aerial yoga instructor, then hiring the doula-tographer, needing a lactation consultant, and then the six weeks of time off from teaching yoga postpartum. At least with student loan or medical debt, there was some finite ending to the balance. But a baby? *Get a real job*, I thought. There was the married couple with over $200K in student loan debt from law school, but the wife stayed at home, and they sent their two kids to private school and only shopped at Whole Foods. Their parents paid the grandkids' tuition, they said. The Whole Foods was nonnegotiable, they said. We'll probably have this debt until we're dead, they said.

Not planning to have children made me feel like my future self had money in the bank.

• • •

"Your dad will pay for college," my mom always promised. I assumed this meant that they had made a plan. A plan that explained those few bad years. Maybe instead of paying child support, he had been putting the money aside in a college fund.

But when we told him I got into NYU, there was no money. Nothing.

"I don't understand, Steve," I said. I hardly ever called him by his name, but it felt like the only leverage I had, to speak as one adult to another.

"I tried, kid," he said.

That's not true, I thought.

You don't even know me well enough to have a nickname for me, I thought.

I felt my teeth vibrating with anger.

My mom and I had to downsize after she finally quit Amway. By the time I was in high school, we'd lost the little two-bedroom rental house and moved into a one-bedroom above a strip mall. She let me have the bedroom. My mom had no credit and Steve wouldn't even cosign my loans. I should have sucked it up and gone to a state school, but that would have been an admission that I was ordinary, not destined for any life other than the one I already knew.

I went to my AP US History teacher and she helped me cobble together my financial aid, with Pell grants and merit scholarships, and tens of thousands of dollars in loans for which she cosigned.

My mom and I lived on the same flavor of hope: that someday our payday would come. We would attract abundance through our positive thinking. Our flaws were our strengths. Our sacrifice had a purpose. Our wrong turns were leading us to the right path. The cycle of circumstances that conspired to keep us broke would be broken.

• • •

John got the Alpine mac and cheese with Gruyère and bacon and onion rings and apple compote and a Diet Coke, and I got the

Rive Gauche with Brie and figs and lobster and a fourth glass of pinot grigio. John moved a stack of books from the coffee table to the floor so there was room for us to eat. I kept thinking our relationship would improve if we could afford a table and chairs, to look into each other's eyes when we talked, instead of at the TV. But there wasn't any room for a table and chairs.

"Your mom called."

"She called you?"

"She said she tried texting you."

I hadn't had time to look at any messages that weren't related to what Evan had done, the question of how much Richual users were aware of, or talking about, what Evan had done, and Devin's defense of what Evan had done.

"She wanted to ask if you needed any refills so she can meet her monthly goal." He handed me a Post-it note, on which he'd scrawled:

True Color Smooth Minerals Powder Foundation Soft Ivory $8.99

Anew Multiperformance Day Cream SPF 25 $22.99

Breathe Again Roll-On $34.99

Forgiveness Essential Oil $70.99

In the bathroom, I had trays of product I never wore. Who wore Avon in New York? Like buying tickets to a friend's fringe theater performance or donating to a GoFundMe, I ordered makeup and skincare products and essential oils from my mom out of pity and obligation.

"I'll call her back after we eat."

"I told her to just order it and you'd send her a check," he said, his mouth full of hot yellow mush.

Thanks, John, I thought. *Thanks for all your help.* My wrists tingled and my hands were pins and needles. This had happened before. It was a symptom of overwork.

"I finished the scene today," John said. "Of the couple eating the turtle."

"I thought you wrote that scene already."

"I had an idea for how it would go, but I wasn't sure if I was right in how I imagined someone would eat a raw turtle. You wouldn't believe what I found on YouTube."

"Please don't show me."

"You know what this means?"

"What?" I said.

"My novel. I'm done. It's ready for you to read. It's eight hundred pages, but I can worry about editing later."

"That's great, babe," I said. I tried to mold my face into a realistic impression of genuine excitement.

I kept my phone next to me on the couch while we ate, just in case it buzzed or rang. This must be how surgeons felt. I might be needed in an emergency. No, working online was worse than being a surgeon. Your career as a surgeon didn't continue in virtual space while you slept or ate breakfast or had sex or shopped at Fairway.

"Are your wrists okay?" John asked. I was staring at the fork in my right hand.

"They hurt," I said, and my eyes filled with tears as soon as I said it.

"Do you want me to feed you like a baby?"

I laughed. "No," I said.

He took his own fork and fed me a bite of golden noodles, cupping one hand under my chin. Right now, there were hundreds of conversations happening that impacted my company's brand, its leadership, my own brand, my reputation. I could force myself to detach, but it was going to get worse before it got better. I envied Khadijah, for whom Richual was just a job, separate from her personal life. Disconnected from her identity. How did she spend her evenings and weekends, all those hours of freedom from labor? I was only thirty-one, but already I missed my twenties, the decade of not knowing any better.

"Maren? Hello?"

"Sorry, what did you say?"

"You're working right now," he said.

"I'm not on my phone. I'm not on my laptop. I'm totally present."

"I can tell you're working in your head. You never take a break, even when you're away from the office."

I brushed away his hand, holding another bite. "You don't even know what happened. Evan was accused of assaulting all these women."

"I saw," John said. "It was all over the news."

"Devin thinks he's innocent," I said.

"Of course she does."

"What does that mean?"

"They're best friends, right?"

A bolt of pain shot through my right wrist. That couldn't be true. I was Devin's best friend. I had an honorary doctorate in her social media footprint. I knew her better than anyone. Not Evan. Evan didn't care about anyone but himself.

"Well, I think he's guilty," I said.

"He's definitely a creep. But did you notice that the worst accusations came from the one source who wants to remain anonymous?"

"What's that supposed to mean?"

"What if some woman made anonymous accusations against me?"

"Why, what you have done?"

"Nothing!"

"Then you don't have anything to worry about!" I yelled. John put his head in his hands. He was like a stuffed animal, harmless, made to be squeezed. He didn't understand what it felt like to be responsible, to carry the burden of making the women's corner of the internet run like a well-moisturized machine.

"I'm sorry," I said. I kissed his forehead so many times I lost count. "I don't mean to stress you out with my work stuff. I shouldn't take it out on you. It's not fair. I'll figure out how to handle it."

I started clearing the dishes. My wineglass was empty. I didn't remember finishing it.

"What are you going to do?" he asked.

"I don't know yet."

"Babe, at least sleep on it," he said. "You'll feel better in the morning."

• • •

Devin and Evan both grew up in New York City. They attended private schools, slept at the same sleepaway camps, and danced at the same bar mitzvahs. They knew the rules of lacrosse and where to get a fake ID on St. Marks. They had parents who understood the added value of Adderall and extortionate SAT tutors, letters of recommendation from notable alumni, paid internships at some corporation where a cousin sits on the board, don't forget the thank-you note. Devin and Evan knew the same cast of characters, including the girl on Lexapro who jumped from the top of her apartment building on the Upper East Side at the end of senior year and no one would cop to being part of the rumor mill that led her to leap, but everyone pitched in to make an epic playlist for the funeral. I'd heard them talk about the aftermath of a violent hazing incident where the attorney explained to the judge his client didn't realize how the alcohol would interact with the medication he took for borderline personality disorder, and about another guy who swore the anal sex in the coed's dorm room was consensual because she let him spend the night, didn't she?, and after he was expelled his parents hired a crisis management consultant to help him write another round of college applications (*don't forget the thank-you note*).

You protected the people who were most like you. Devin had to defend Evan. That was the code. Their live-in nannies raised them to be Good People, to do the right thing and tell the truth about it, but if for any reason you couldn't do the right thing, or if your idea of the right thing was different from mine, or if you did the wrong thing and there was no way you could tell the truth and still save yourself, then Mommy and Daddy had money for extravagant arbitration, crisis comms, an educational consultant, a spirit quest, a new diagnosis, sixty days in-patient, an affluenza defense.

But I wasn't from their world. I didn't have to follow their code.

After dinner, I strapped on my beige wrist braces from CVS. Then I searched through the weekend bag I hadn't unpacked after Evan's house, until I found the photos of the two women, one in the red wig, one blond. Neither was Kimberly Hartsong.

I googled *Rachelle Tanaka*.

Her LinkedIn came up. She had a sweet oval face that looked familiar, but it didn't match either of the women.

One of them had to be the ex-girlfriend from the article. She wasn't a nobody. She had a face, a body, a brain, a heart. And he was just going to get away with what he'd done to her? Because she was anonymous? I could post these images on the internet right now. I could say I had been inside Evan's house and found evidence of his misconduct. I wasn't afraid of him. He should have been afraid of me. I was holding a straight flush.

Are you home? I texted. There's something I have to show you.

Foundress Summit

Power in 2017:
Are We There Yet?

8:15 a.m. (Ignite session) What's Your Story, Who's Your Audience, and Why Should They Give a Shit? with Clementine Hopkins-Halloway of Dragg & Dropp

Are you telling your brand's story or is your brand telling the story of you? Reclaim the power of storytelling by tapping into experiences that only you can share—let those experiences shed light on the universal truths that align with your core values and then communicate them. Find out which stories are actually interesting to people and which are actually not, from Clementine Hopkins-Halloway, the creator of *EDM Sober House* and *Hit Me Baby: My MMA Fiancé*.

9:00 a.m. (Keynote) Our Bodies, Our Selfies: A State of the Union of Wellness Address and Fireside Chat, sponsored by Richual

When it comes to wellness, *hygiene* and *self-care* are two major buzzwords. What if you could be both *clean* and *taken care of*? Join Devin Avery, cofoundress and chief executive officer of Richual, and Arianna Tran, foundress and chief visionary officer of S'Wipe, for an illuminating conversation about cleansing our minds and bodies, even while we ascend the career ladder. *Light breakfast will be served.*

10:15 a.m. (Session A) Pitch Pageant: Who Is the Fairest of Them All?, sponsored by Finishing Touch

Contestants have ninety seconds to deliver their pitches in the video booth sponsored by the As Seen on TV Finishing Touch Lumina Personal Hair Remover. Mark Cuban, Chris Sacca, Ashton Kutcher, and Evan Wiley will review and score the pitches based on personality, presentation, appearance, and minimum viable product, via livestream. Winners will be announced tomorrow on Twitter. Follow us @FoundressSummit and #FoundressSummit17! *Advance sign-up required.*

10:15 a.m. (Session B) What on Earth Were You Put on This Earth to Do and Is Your Personal Brand Reflecting Your Calling?

Can you describe your world-changing manifesto in three words? Is your LinkedIn photo in harmony with your professional tagline? Before you take a single further step in your career, take the time to align what it is you want to do with your brand across social channels.

12:00 p.m. (Lunch) We've Got Issues

When's the last time you slept through the night? Can an anti-inflammation diet slow down the aging process? By the time you're thirty, how much retirement savings should you have?

Today, women entrepreneurs are doing more than just raising capital. They're also raising awareness about serious issues that affect women all over the country: underbanked millennials and the true costs of having no retirement savings, the latest scientific research on why we need to sleep at night, the delicate art of negotiating for a higher salary without sounding selfish, and the superfoods that promote longevity so you can live long enough for the compound interest to grow in those retirement accounts!

2:00 p.m. (Session A) Restorative Tarot for Times of Burnout

Have you drawn a Hanged Man card on the question of your life? Learn about, and reclaim, the archetypes that promote healing, wisdom, and guidance for your venture.

2:00 p.m. (Session B) She's a Friend of the Pod

With over 100,000 downloads every week, the Profiteering Mavens have built up a devoted fanbase of creative entrepreneurs seeking no bullshit advice for growing their side hustles in the gig economy. Find out their exact cold emailing formula that has landed them guests such as Marie Forleo, Audrey Gelman, Danielle LaPorte, and Amanda Chantal Bacon.

3:30 p.m. (Panel) Film Gives Back

What is it really like in Africa? Hear from the actresses who've been to the country, what they saw in terms of malnutrition and vaccination rates, and how it deepened their understanding of humanity and prepared them for some of the grittiest roles of their careers. From gaining twenty pounds to play a postpartum character, to playing a woman who has to overcome how differently abled she is, these actresses are making waves and giving back. *Exact lineup TBA.*

Foundress Summit is a ticketed event. Every attendee must have a ticket. To be eligible for a ticket, you must be a woman age 18 or over. Email us for a list of recommended childcare providers, or if you need a map to the lactation room.

Devin

The lighting in the lobby was not great. Very fluorescent, very awake-inducing. The skin on the back of my hands looked washed out, like raw fish. *Let me see those hands . . . in the air: how many of you . . . think of yourself . . . as heroes . . . in someone else's . . . story?* The morning session had already begun—I could hear it from behind a flimsy black partition at one end of the lobby. *And how many of you . . . think of yourself as heroes . . . in . . .*

A staff member in black jeans and a black crop top that said "The Future Is Foundre$$" was shushing a group of conference attendees standing in the lobby in bodycon dresses, saying that they couldn't talk *here*; they had to talk over *there* in a special room, because the sound was carrying over into the session. One woman, in a jade-colored dress with a gold back zipper, said, "I didn't pay twenty-five-hundred dollars to be quarantined in the overflow room!" The staff member was apologizing and explaining that it wasn't an overflow room—it was a *conversation corner*.

I had to wait my turn in line at the VIP registration desk, behind an attendee who was complaining that something in her swag bag wasn't the flavor she wanted, or had an ingredient she was allergic to, or that her friend got something in her swag bag that she didn't also receive, something expensive.

"I don't want you to think that I'm one of those entitled women—"

"Oh, not at all," the staffer said, holding up a finger to me that she'd just be a minute. "It's only that we stuffed, I mean prepared, the gift bags at a different venue, so unfortunately I'm not totally sure if I have the product to swap out for you right this moment."

"I paid a premium for this VIP badge and honestly you're not making me feel very VIP at all right now."

"Would you like to leave your contact info and someone will follow up on Monday?"

"I *know* Michelle," the woman said, digging through her handbag for a business card. Michelle was the foundress of Foundress. "Michelle *knows* me. We were at Brearley together. I was actually supposed to moderate the Film Gives Back panel, but at the last minute Michelle said it would look better to have someone who's more diverse."

"That's amazing," said the staffer, checking a notification on her phone. Her nails were painted in alternating pink and gray, to match the brand. Her name badge read "Delancey." "I'll be sure to pass along what happened, and again I'm so sorry about the mix-up."

Finally, it was my turn. "And you must be Devin," she said.

Is there any greater high in life than being recognized? From under the registration table, Delancey pulled a pink nylon weekender bag that was at least twice the size of all the other swag bags I'd seen. The number 25 was written in sequins on one side and there was a sparkly unicorn head on the other.

"Is that like the number of children who get to eat when I use this bag?" I asked.

"Oh, maybe! I thought it was the number of pounds."

As I slung the unicorn body bag over one shoulder, something heavy and cold inside slammed against the side of my rib cage.

"Can I get someone to help this speaker with her VIP satchel? Hey!" Delancey yelled at a staffer in black who was wearing wrist braces and carrying a velvet wingback chair, by herself, across the lobby.

It wasn't a staff member. It was Maren. She set the chair down by the registration table and slung my bag over her own shoulder like a good boyfriend.

"Did you get a new job?" I asked.

"I'm performing manual labor for the rich and undernourished. It's my cardio." She blotted the sweat on her forehead with the back of a brace.

"You shouldn't be lifting anything if you're having a repetitive stress injury flare."

"I lift from the legs," Maren said. "C'mon, I'll show you where your talk is. I got here early and it was a clusterfuck, so I started moving furniture."

Maren was at her best when she could shine like a diamond against the rough of everyone else's incompetence.

"Should there be a RichualCon?" she asked. "We'd do such a better job. Don't you think? What even is this venue?"

"It's the law school."

"I know it's the law school," Maren said, leading me through a banquet room with Oriental rugs and oil paintings of fat bald white men in three-piece suits from olden times. "Does the ambiance scream 'empower women' to you?"

She pulled aside a heavy black curtain and showed me some kind of makeshift tech booth with wires running everywhere and, in one corner, a mirrored vanity table and coat rack.

"What's your name?" Maren barked at the ambiguously gendered person sitting at the sound board.

"Topher."

"Do you work here, Topher?"

"Yeah, I'm the tech."

My phone buzzed. It was a text from Maren, who was standing inches away from me: Should we ask what their preferred pronouns are?

🙂, I texted back.

"Topher," Maren said, "I'm Maren and my pronouns are she and her. This is Devin. She is moderating the breakfast conversation. Is it cool if she leaves her bags back here?"

Topher gave a thumbs-up.

I made Maren take a selfie of us in the good light of the vanity mirror—her arms were longer. Good morning from #Foundress-Summit17!!! I posted to Richual. Here with my business bestie before I interview the inspiring @ForRealAriannaTran about @s-wipe. So blessed to be here. 🌟 💀 🙏

"Hey, can I talk to you about something?" Maren asked.

"Sure, what's up?"

"This'll only take two minutes." She unwrapped her wrist braces. "I'm going to give you a real hug that's not from a cyborg."

Maren held me to her like a child, but it was hard to relax because it was too early in the morning for so much intimate touch. She smelled like black coffee and onion bagel and cool cucumber antiperspirant. Her core radiated heat. She spoke in a low, quiet voice.

"I just wanted to tell you how grateful I am that you're my business partner and how proud I am of the work we're doing. I feel like . . . do we even take the time to pause and reflect on how many women we've helped by giving them permission to put themselves first? Do we even make time to celebrate our achievement?"

"I don't know. I thought we did?"

"Sometimes it feels like we're just going from one crisis to another, so I wanted to just take this moment to say *you're doing a great job*."

"Maren, this is getting a little too romantic."

I felt her big laugh in her heart chakra and then she let me go. My highlighter left a sparkly smear across the front of her dress.

"You're important to me," she said, her forehead wrinkled with concern. "That's all. Richual is important to me. And not just me—but lots of other people, too. We're counting on you."

"Oh my god, do you have the BRCA gene?"

"No, I'm not sick. I'm not going anywhere. But you're the face, Devin. You've always been the face. When people think of Richual, they think of your selfies. And that's why I think you should be the one to read this." She was holding a folded piece of paper.

"Read what?"

"Let me back up," Maren said. "So I went over to Evan's apartment last night."

No. That wasn't possible. I was texting him after my class and he said he was too tired to see anyone and I said, No problem I understand. I was so understanding. I gave him so much space. Why don't you make some chamomile tea and take a couple drops of that cannabis tincture you got in Seattle? He couldn't even tell me that she was there?

"Why?" I asked.

"Because it's not fair," Maren said. "Why should Richual have to put out a statement about Evan? Why can't Evan speak for himself? Why are women always the ones burdened with the emotional labor?"

The reason we were in this position in the first place was because of women. Rachelle Tanaka was jealous of our valuation. Kimberly Hartsong was no one's favorite bachelorette; she had a ridiculous bird phobia; her viewership numbers were pathetic. But now she'd reentered the conversation. Everyone felt sorry for her. This drama was taking away from what today was really supposed to be about—women's empowerment.

"I got Evan to write this statement," Maren said.

> There is a lot of pain in this country right now and marginalized groups such as women are hurting worst of all. I have my own side of what happened, but rather than make excuses or apologize, I would rather decenter my own experience and

make space for those who don't have a voice because that's something I believe in.

"What does this even mean?" I asked. I read it again: *Marginalized groups such as women. Decenter my experience. I believe in.* I recognized his handwriting, but those were Maren's words.

"Before you even start the conversation with Arianna, you should read it," she said. "It's the elephant in the room. If you don't acknowledge the accusations against Evan, they're going to bulldoze you in the Q and A. He's on the judges panel for the livestreamed pitch competition."

"So?"

"*So* I overheard attendees complaining about it this morning, and asking Michelle to find a replacement. Women are really mad about it online."

People were always comparing the internet to high school. But in high school, the mean girls just wanted to ruin your reputation in the short term. Online, people wanted to destroy your reputation for life, so you could never work again under your own brand.

"Do you want me to read it? I'll read it."

"That's great. Why don't I just go home and you can rearrange the furniture and run the sound booth and interview Arianna and read The Statement and show everyone how good you are at everything, better than anyone else, ever?"

"Don't be pissed at *me*," Maren said. "I didn't do anything."

Topher was staring at us. "Five minutes," they said.

"You don't even know Evan. You had one conversation with

him and you think you understand what's happening? There's a lot you don't know, Maren. *A lot.* Like the fact that we've been seeing each other. Did he tell you that?"

She blinked. The paper fell from her hand and stuck to a piece of black electrical tape on the floor. "Seeing each other in what way exactly?"

"You know."

"No, Devin, actually I don't."

"He's my boyfriend. I just didn't know how to tell you." I could tell how true this sounded by the crestfallen look on her face.

"You should have told me sooner."

"When? At the office? Because that's the only place I ever see you anymore?"

"Maybe you could have found some time to squeeze me in between your Botox and your brow-shaping appointments."

I almost felt sorry for her. We both knew that the reason Foundress invited me to moderate the conversation with Arianna was because of the way I looked. The time and money I spent on my appearance gave me an advantage. Maren would never admit this. It meant we weren't equals.

"I don't understand why you had to keep it a secret," she said. "That's all."

"Just because I didn't do something the way you would have wanted me to do it doesn't mean I did it the wrong way, okay? And now I have to go."

"This conversation isn't over. We're putting a pin in this." She picked up the statement and pressed it into my hand.

I checked my makeup and strode toward the front of the banquet room, imagining summertime at the country house—Evan saying, *Mom, I'm bringing someone*—the two of us sharing a hammock, taking a photo of my bare feet next to his, posting it to Richual. Picking blueberries. Catching fireflies in our hands. Roleplaying sexy drowning victim/lifeguard by the pool. Four hundred women were seated at round tables in the audience, waiting to hear what I had to say. For once, I won. I told Maren something she didn't already know.

. . .

Arianna was half-Vietnamese and half-Scandinavian and one-eighth Sephardic Jew. She was six foot two in heels and lost the baby weight in sixty days by going keto. I estimated her pants size at a 26 long. In 2015, her company was nearly destroyed by a scandal over whether or not the estrogen ingredient in her restorative eye serum was truly vegan since it was taken from the urine of pregnant horses, but they survived (the company, not the horses) by pivoting to wipes. None of this was in the official bio on the conference website; it's extra research I did on my own on her social accounts and Wikipedia.

Arianna was no slouch. She was wearing a wool crepe sheath with flutter three-quarter sleeves in a shade of pink pearl and she found a way to perch in the wingback chair, smooth as a headless department store mannequin, without wrinkling her dress or revealing too much leg. I predicted she would be wearing a dress, so I went for a herringbone pantsuit.

Ready? I mouthed and she gave me a wink.

"How's everybody doing this morning?" A few women put down the spoons from their overnight oats to clap. There was one loud *whoop* from the back of the room. "This is the moment we've all been waiting for. I know I have. I'm here this morning with Arianna Tran, foundress of S'Wipe, to talk about money and power."

"Devin, I am seriously your biggest fan! Can I be on your shine squad?" From the way her head was angled, it was unclear whether this question was addressed to the audience or to me.

"This is actually the first time we're meeting IRL," I said. "And yes. You can."

Arianna turned to me. "You know what I just realized?"

"What?"

"It's kind of funny that we're having this talk in a room where every oil painting on the wall is of a man."

"I love that you just *said* that," I said, smiling through my déjà vu. *Did Maren tell her to say that?*

"I hope I didn't just jeopardize my speaking fee!"

Laughter rolled through the crowd.

"For those who are new to your work, maybe we could start by you telling everybody a little bit about your background."

"Absolutely." There were two male event photographers documenting every time we crossed or uncrossed our legs, switched the microphone from one hand to the other, brushed our hair from our shoulders. "To be honest, I grew up working-class in Cupertino. Both my parents worked, like, a lot. My dad is an anesthesiologist and my mom is an econ professor at Stanford.

When I tell people I'm from Cupertino, they assume I grew up immersed in tech and startup culture, but I really had zero exposure. Everything I've built, I built it myself."

"How did you get started in business?"

"All my friends in high school—their parents were buying them cars. I wanted a Jetta so bad, you guys! I also had asthma as a kid so I was always different, an outsider. Raise your hand if you've ever felt like you needed to look different or have different stuff or even *breathe* different to fit in. Don't be shy! That's all of us. I thought maybe having the right car would help me fit in. Because my parents worked so much, they instilled in me that work ethic. This was during the dot-com boom and I got a job doing sales after school and on the weekends for a box website and made twenty thousand dollars in commissions. I was only a junior."

"Dropbox?"

"Pre-Dropbox. A website that sold boxes. Our company supplied boxes to other companies, but instead of ordering from a catalog you could order from our website."

Arianna must have been way older than I thought. I couldn't help scanning her face for what had been filled and lifted. We were losing our audience. The bubble burst before most of these women got their first periods.

"Let's actually stay on that topic of money for a minute," I said, checking my notes. "Now that your company has expanded from nontoxic makeup remover wipes to nontoxic baby wipes to a patented, uniquely biodegradable flushable wipe you call the 'Number 1 for Number 2' organic adult wipe on the market, can you tell us something you learned along the way about negotiation and closing the deal?"

Arianna set her mic in her lap and just stared at me, expressionless, like I'd said something borderline offensive and she wanted me to reflect on it.

I tried again. "Sorry, I mean I was just wondering if you had any negotiation tips for the women in the audience who are negotiating with suppliers or even, like, in an interview."

She didn't even blink. Should I not have said "flushable"? Should I not have said "women"? Should I have said "people"? "Women and people?" *Women are people. All people are human beings.* My pits were sweating, even though the room was cold. The fireplace behind us was a barren showpiece. All eyes—dark eyes and light eyes, lined eyes and nude eyes, and eyes framed by false lashes—were on me, begging me to make this moment with our elder less excruciatingly awkward. I remembered when Evan wanted 50 percent equity and how Maren had laughed like a cold dead fish and said, *You must be shitting me,* and Evan saying, *Hey, this is a negotiation,* and Maren saying, *Last I checked you didn't have the authority of a vagina,* and Evan looking to me, all casual, saying, *Are you sure this is the cunt you want to be going into business with?* How I said, *Yes, this is the cunt I choose,* and he said, *I just want you both to be sure. This is the easy part. It doesn't get any easier from here.* We gave him 20 percent and the third seat on our board.

Finally, Arianna picked her mic back up. "Don't speak," she said.

"I'm sorry," I said automatically.

"Stop apologizing, Devin," she said, leaning in to squeeze one of my knees, before turning back to the adoring crowd. "This is a lesson for everybody. After you put out, you shut up. You put what you fucking *want* on the table, and then you sit quietly until they make their fucking *counteroffer*."

I was afraid that if I said anything right then, I might start crying, so I put my mic in my lap and started a round of applause that, blessedly, everyone joined in on. Maren was standing at the back of the room near the doors, giving me a thumbs-up. I was overwhelmed at the amount of relief I felt seeing her there. She was still on my team. We were still a team.

"Wow, that was *so* powerful." I took a deep breath. "Switching gears, maybe we can talk about what you've learned about balancing being a mom with being an entrepreneur."

"I actually hate the word *balance*," Arianna said. "I prefer *blend*."

"Can you describe what that blend looks like?"

"I'm just speaking for myself, but for me, I have three kids. If you send me a Twitter DM, I might not have time to look at it until I'm pumping at the office. My assistant is at my house at six in the morning so we can do email while I hit the Peloton. The nanny has the day off on Sundays and for some reason it takes the kids forever to fall asleep—"

Maren was waving her phone at me broadly, like a flag. *Stop*, I mouthed.

Look, she mouthed back, gesturing at her phone, looking at the screen and back at me. I shook my head. I was not delivering that statement, not now. No way.

"—when I'm putting them to bed, so maybe I'll be cuddling

with them and reviewing an audit of our market segmentation on my tablet or something. My work is my life and my life is my work. And my kids are all of that and more."

"That's incredible," I said, shuffling through my notes for a good follow-up. My question on the postpartum body dysmorphia she chronicled on Instagram didn't seem appropriate. I could have asked her about her next venture with breast wipes, but I thought I should save that one for the end.

"What is something that makes you hopeful?" I asked.

"This. Women. Women speaking up. Women getting loud. Women talking to each other. Women saying, *This really happened to me.* Women sharing space to talk about times they failed, but also about the times they succeeded . . . Are we at time?"

She was looking at me and I was looking at her and that's when I saw, over Arianna's shoulder, the crowd. They seemed to appear everywhere at once: women dressed in all black, standing at the back and sides of the room. They were all wearing white sheet masks. The masks were one size fits all. On some women, they sagged around the chin. On others, they didn't quite reach the hairline. No one had a nose. At first, that was the creepiest part of all—the complete lack of noses. Just a white flap to ventilate the nostrils. A gash in the mask for a mouth. They looked like burn victims.

They began to disperse throughout the crowd, carrying brightly colored bundles under their arms. I searched for Maren, but she was gone.

"It appears we have some S'Wipe samples for everyone," I started to say, even while Arianna was shaking her head at me, concerned. The women in masks weren't wearing Foundress-branded T-shirts. They weren't staff. I reached for my phone, but it wasn't even on me—it was in the closet. I felt like I had forgotten how to breathe.

"Melissa? Is Melissa here?" I was still gripping my mic. "I don't mean Melissa. I mean Michelle! Security? Sorry, you guys, I think there's been some slight miscommunication in the programming—"

"Hey, that's my foot!" a woman yelled in the front row.

"Then move your fucking foot," one of the creepy ghosts yelled back. A cyclone of gasps at the table. At the next table, two twentysomethings clutched their Kate Spade bags to their chests like armor. Something violent was about to happen. Somewhere, someone was crying. Maybe they had guns. Maybe this was the end of my life. A senseless mass murder of all the influencers they could find together in the same room. At least Maren and I would die together.

A masked woman walked directly toward me, one naked boob sticking defiantly out of her blouse, an actual baby attached to the nipple. I was cornered. I couldn't run. I would have had to run right through them. There were at least thirty women, maybe forty. Some of the masks were starting to slip off and the protestors were frantically trying to keep them stuck on, even tilting their faces up at the ceiling so it almost looked like they were praying when they unrolled the pink and green beach towels, the beach towels from my own office, the beach towels that said "Believe Victims" and once their flags had unfurled, they began chanting the words.

You Must Change
Your Life

Maren

According to the internet, I was right.

Does your friend only talk about her relationship at a very surface level, without going into detail about what it's like when the two are alone together?

Is she attached to her phone when she's away from him, just in case she might miss a message and risk his anger?

Does she seem apologetic for her partner's behavior?

Does she make excuses on his behalf?

Devin was the bird in the wall, flapping her wings desperately as I tried to identify the source of her entrapment. How had I missed the signs for so long? Had she wanted me to notice? Were all her excuses for his behavior, her denial, cries for my help?

She was staring out the window of the cab, lost in her own

movie, sniffling intermittently, while I googled what to do. I was taking her home. At least with me, she was safe.

Everything had happened so fast that I only had time to react, like Tom Cruise but taller, basically invincible, my wrist braces my shield against the women standing between me and the fireplace where Devin stood trembling, repeating the names of every important person she knew into a microphone, hoping someone else could fix what went so wrong. My feet crunched over granola crumbs and slipped on goop from fallen face masks. The newly nude-faced protestors reached into their backpacks for scarves and handkerchiefs, to hide their refreshed complexions.

"Hey hey! Ho ho! Believe victims or you've got to go! Hey hey! Ho ho!"

All the conference attendees had their phones out, documenting that they were, like, actually there. Even the women rushing toward the exits ran backward in order to take some video for their Instagram story. One of the event photographers was standing on the buffet table, straddling a platter of mini croissants, so he could get an aerial view of the chaos.

They were protesting Devin as if she were some major corporation that had profited from the transatlantic slave trade. They were protesting against a system of violence and oppression. But Devin wasn't systemic. She and I were just two women who had started a company together—from scratch. We had leaned in. This was America. Everyone was supposed to be on our side.

"Devin, we have to go now," I told her, taking the mic from her and setting it on the chair. Two security guards from the law school were escorting Arianna out. *So sorry*, she mouthed. *Yikes!* This was our problem, not hers.

"I looked for you!" Devin cried. "I looked for you and you weren't there." I had never seen her so small, like a child separated from her mother at a carnival.

"I was here the whole time," I said.

"What do they want from me? I'll read the statement if you think I should read the statement."

I grabbed her hand and pulled her toward a fire exit at the back of the banquet room.

"No crying," I said. "Not until we're in the cab."

Does your friend seem on edge around her partner?

Is she giving up activities that once seemed important to her?

Is she physically isolated from her friends?

Is she lying to you?

"Do you have any booze?" I asked, searching her kitchen cabinets, but finding only tapioca flour, teff flour, chia seeds, Medjool dates, mung beans, and three dozen individual servings of unsweetened organic applesauce.

"Check the wine fridge," Devin said.

Of course. The wine fridge.

I selected a discreetly labeled bottle of pinot noir that, if I had to guess, cost more than eleven dollars. At Evan's apartment the night before, he had offered me a drink and I had refused on principle. The principle of not taking anything from him that wasn't a sacrifice. *I'm surprised. I thought you drank*, he said. *Not anymore*, I told him. I could almost see the new me when I said it. Then I stood at his marble kitchen island like a sentry, dictating what he should write in his statement. After I left, I was sure he'd immediately destroyed the pictures I traded in exchange, lighting them on fire with a match on his wraparound terrace, telling himself he was a victim of blackmail, not a perpetrator of sexual violence.

If he laid one finger on Devin, I would kill him. Not literally, because I knew enough about mass incarceration to not want to go there, but I would ruin his life somehow, using the internet, until he rued the day he met me.

"It's nine in the morning," Devin said, when I handed her a glass.

"It's ten fifteen."

Devin's apartment had the spacious dimensions of a yoga studio, with bamboo floors and windowsill succulents, an altar to Lakshmi and Mary-Kate Olsen, and more props than furniture. I sat on a meditation cushion, hunched over bent knees in my tight dress.

"How did they even get the towels from my office?" She was lying on the couch, looking as pale and fragile as a peeled banana.

"You know as much as I do," I said, raising the bottle. "Cheers. To women supporting other women."

Devin swirled the pinot in her glass and sniffed. I took a swig directly from the bottle and scrolled through the FoundressSummit17 hashtag on Twitter.

@FoundressSummit are you providing refunds for those of us who didn't sign up to attend a protest this morning?

@FoundressSummit how was that prof development???

@FoundressSummit I flew in from Charlotte just to have the opportunity to meet @ForRealAriannaTran and I'm soooooo disappointed. Can I get an e-intro?

Everyone's talking about Devin Avery's misogyny but is anyone talking about how @FoundressSummit doesn't allow nursing infants? Journos, DM me for my story.

Due to a scheduling conflict, @VerifiablyEvanWiley will not be able to participate in today's Pitch Pageant. All other programming is ON, as planned.

"Where's *my* phone?"

"In your bag," I said.

"My bag is in the green room."

"Shit."

"It doesn't matter," she said, taking off her blazer and turning it into a tent to cover her entire face and chest.

"I'll send an intern."

"It's better this way. This way I don't have to know."

It was mind-blowing to me that she could just opt out from the live feed of reactions to the shitshow we'd both lived through. There was a nine-second video of Devin's facial expressions— puzzled, pissed, pained, panicked—as she watched the protestors, with twelve hundred retweets already. Nothing I ever did in the nonprofit space ever went so viral. In the attention economy, thoughtful solutions had so little value. What you did wrong was more engaging than what you did right. While she lay corpselike on the couch, her phone a limb lost on the battlefield, Devin was reaching the pinnacle of internet fame. Her face had become a meme.

> Tell your friend you're concerned about her. Say, what's up with you lately? I never see you anymore. Say, I love you.
>
> Say, I'll always be here for you.
>
> Listen.
>
> Make sure she knows it's not her fault.

I put my phone screen down on the coffee table and sat next to Devin's legs. Now I couldn't look at her body without thinking of him, where he had touched her, how he might have violated her.

"Help me understand," I finally said.

"Understand what."

"What it's like being Evan's girlfriend."

"Are you joking?"

"I really want to know," I said. I thought of all those nights I spent at the office, sending emails, staring at spreadsheets until my eyes crossed, adding emojis to the interns' idiotic posts on Slack so they felt appreciated, while the two of them were together, that whole time, leading a life that didn't include me. I felt like the hired help, the virtual assistant in another time zone.

"Whatever I say, you're going to twist it around to make him the bad guy."

"Is that why you never talk about him?"

She pulled down the jacket to reveal her face. The color was coming back to her cheeks. "We're very private people. We just like being at home together, like you and John. I don't have to post every part of my life on social."

"This is different. This is me. I'm not a digital platform. If you met someone you were totally crazy about, I'd want you to tell me."

"So you could stalk them online."

"So I could stalk them online," I repeated, and this made Devin laugh. I drank from the bottle.

"I think I should go somewhere," she said, rubbing her eyes. I couldn't tell if she was still laughing or about to start crying. "To find out what's wrong with me. Like rehab."

"Rehab for what?"

"Like a detox."

"You're already the queen of detox," I said. "You need whatever the opposite of detox is. You need retox."

I held the wineglass to her mouth.

"This is awkward, but I have to ask, so drink up. Has Evan ever been physically violent with you?"

"He's not like that. You *know* him."

"Is that what he told you to say?"

"It's not Evan, it's me. There's something wrong with *me*. I think I might have burnout."

No you don't, I thought. *That's what I have.*

How was I supposed to succeed in my role as the concerned friend in the "so you think your friend might be in an abusive

relationship" script when Devin kept deflecting? Devin didn't
have body dysmorphia; she had *celiac disease*. She wasn't lazy; she
was *mindful*. She wasn't bulimic; she was *cleansing her colon*. She
wasn't a victim—just *burned out*. She worked *so hard*. She just
needed *a break*.

I put my hands on her ankles and held her to the couch.

"You don't work hard enough to have burnout," I said.

She blinked at me.

"Look at our lives. You leave work at six on the dot to take a
thirty-five-dollar aerobics class. You live *here*. You have a *wine
fridge*. You subscribe to a fresh juice delivery service. You 'unplug'
on weekends and put your phone in a special handwoven basket.
Look at me. I'm wearing a dress that makes me look like a sausage
because it was forty percent off. Look at my—" I held up my
wrists. "My hands are numb right now."

"What about my eczema!"

"You *know* I put in more hours than you at the office, but you
won't admit it because you think your beauty and grooming routines should count as work."

She stood up so fast she kicked me and her jacket flew off. Her
arms were pale, unblemished, delicately defined in the Tracy Anderson mode. The scent of her body was sweat and period blood,
hardly masked by her useless natural deodorant.

"I just think if we're being radically honest with one another—"

"Fuck you, Maren."

"Tell me what's really going on with Evan and then I can
help you."

"I don't need your help. I'm not the sick one. You're the one who thinks she deserves a trophy for having no life. Good job, Maren, here's a sticker for answering all your emails instead of sleeping. Congratulations on all the weekends you've spent at the office alone. It's pathetic. You think everyone should feel sorry for you just because you don't know how to take care of yourself."

She was wrong. I wanted so much more than a trophy or sympathy—I wanted damages. I wanted financial compensation for working the hardest and sacrificing the most to the cause: my own health and well-being. I wanted Devin to die and leave me her apartment in her will. No, that would take too long. I wanted her to Venmo me $10,000 right now. *You deserve this. You've been a good girl. You've helped so many people.* With more money, maybe I could be a beautiful, skinny bitch, too. What a luxury, to be able to devote so much time and attention to your body's inputs and outputs, to be able to say your biggest flaw is your perfectionism. I took a long swig from the bottle, looking her right in the eye, daring her to name my problem out loud.

"I get it," she said, refilling her glass from the refrigerator water dispenser. "I'm not as stupid as you think I am."

I didn't say anything.

"You think I'm just a walking selfie. You're wondering why I was interviewing Arianna this morning, and not you. You're like, *Why do we need her again?*"

"That's not true. I do need you."

"Your feminism"—she hiccupped—"is pretending you don't think less of other women, but you're full of shit. You think less of me."

Something had happened to her. When I first met Devin, she

was ambitious and effervescent. Her desk at work was covered in unicorn plush toys and bouquets of pink flowers and books about being boss. She went after every project with the confidence that she would figure it all out as she went along. I wasn't sure how long she'd been dating Evan, but he had efficiently sucked out all her life force, her self-esteem. He'd damaged *us*.

This was the moment when I should have completed the game of telephone and told her to love herself the way other people loved her. The way I loved her. She couldn't see it.

"Hey, Devin," I said. "I didn't mean to make you so upset."

I followed her to the bathroom, but she slammed the door in my face. I listened to the sounds of her puke hitting the toilet water. She didn't even turn on the faucet. She wanted me to hear.

Khadijah

Are you sure I'm allowed to be in here?" Adam asked, gesturing at a three-tier cake made of boxes of organic cotton tampons that a company sent over as a thank-you for writing branded content that was so good they were going to use our words as an endorsement in their next ad campaign: "Absorbent AF."

I knew that no one would be at the office. Devin and Maren were both at a conference. Chloé had called in sick. Diana was MIA. Katelyn left a Post-it on my desk to say she was going for a coffee run, but it was 10:30 and she still wasn't back.

A couple of the girls from marketing recognized Adam from photos I'd posted of us on Richual.

"Has anyone ever told you that you look like Jesus?" one said.

"Wow, thank you," he said, and winked at me.

He'd come into the city for my twenty-week scan. My white OB liked him more than me and she wasn't polite enough to hide it. They were having a conversation about Linda Ronstadt's influence on the longevity of Warren Zevon's career, while I waited for her to look at my fetus and tell me everything that might possibly go wrong so I could prepare myself.

"The baby is in the breech position now, but there's still plenty of time for the baby to turn. It's something we'll continue to monitor."

"And if the baby stays like that, I'll have to have a C-section, right?" I asked. "I don't want a C-section."

"Like I said, we'll continue to wait and see. Nothing to worry about yet," she said.

Adam squeezed my hand. His grip was warm and firm, an anchor.

"Everything You Ever Wanted to Know About Giving Birth Vaginally but Were Afraid to Ask," I thought, self-soothing the only way I knew how, by translating my anxiety into content. "Are the Organic Skin Care Products You're Putting on Your Face Safe for the Baby in Your Womb?" "So You're Pregnant and You Just Ate Two Bites of Bleu Cheese: One Woman's Story." "Here Are the Symptoms of Preeclampsia, the Life-Threatening Disorder Kim Kardashian West Knows All Too Well."

My legs were so restless they felt haunted. Even bracketed by pillows, I woke up throughout the night, thinking about how I wasn't getting enough sleep. Maybe I was just lonely. As much as Adam assured me he was there for me, here for this, I needed him to show me. I yawned constantly, trying to unpop my ears. Pregnancy was not something I could compartmentalize, like a hobby or a grudge.

Wherever I browsed online, I was seeing ads for Stretch Marks

Survival Kit, Prenatal Cradle belly band, Organic Nipple Butter. There was no end to what I could buy to change my body or keep my body from changing or heal my body from a change.

My mother said I was spending too much time in internet forums, letting strangers tell me what was normal and what wasn't, instead of asking someone who'd known me my whole life.

"You haven't been pregnant in more than twenty-five years," I told her on FaceTime.

"You think we did it different back then?"

"It's not that. It's how much information I'm expected to know now, just because I have access to it. Do you think I should hire a birth coach?"

"Say that again?"

Serious question @ 28 weeks, one forum headline read. **I was 100 pounds when I got pregnant and I'm 113 now. Dr. says this is normal, but do I look huge in this pic? Be honest!**

I took a screenshot for Maren. Richual was missing out on this market segment.

Adam was on his hands and knees, fixing a wobbly leg on my desk with the Swiss army knife he carried in his pocket. The marketing girls and I watched from above.

"What else can he do?" one of the girls—Marisa—asked.

"He builds tiny houses," I told her, just to watch her jaw fall. She took out her phone.

"Is it okay if I take a picture of this for our main channel?"

Adam said sure. But then Marisa's face darkened.

"Oh no," she said. "Look." She opened a new tab on my computer and showed me the headline: "Women's Empowerment

Summit Interrupted by Protestors Who Demand Justice for Victims of Richual Founder."

"That's not even right," I said. "Evan's an investor, not a
founder."

We all watched a nine-second video of Devin's face crumpling
like a paper bag. I felt mortified on her behalf. I nudged Marisa
out of the way so I could sit at the steering wheel of my own vehicle. Who were the protestors? "A crowd of women in coordinated
outfits and masks," it said. Adam was still underneath the desk,
looking up at me, confused. In another window, I looked at the
live tracking of our user stats. They were dropping precipitously.
We were getting dozens of account deactivations a minute.

"Find Katelyn," I told Marisa. "She has to demand a cor-
rection."

"She's not here."

"That's why I said *find her*," I snapped.

I clicked through the slideshow attached to the article. There
was Arianna Tran making Devin laugh in a wingback chair.
There was a white woman seated in the front row smiling with
tears in her eyes, her hands clasped over her heart. Then I saw the
masked activists. I kept clicking as their masks melted off their
faces. I recognized two of them right away from their profile photos on Slack. NicoletteLee and Aja_dontgothere. Shit. There was
our intern Diana. There was a woman who looked just like Gili
nursing a baby.

Well that was an absolute nightmare , Maren texted. I'm sure
you saw.

I signed into the *Stay Woke, Y'all* Slack channel. I hadn't checked it since the news broke about Evan—it didn't seem like a very high priority, but what I'd missed was all their planning. As I scrolled, I pieced it together. Once the Richual press release went out in Evan's defense, all the New York–based users decided how they would take us down. Diana rose to the challenge of matching their outrage word for word. **I will not have my labor further exploited by a company funded by a sexual predator and led by his sycophant,** she wrote. First they would disrupt the conference and confront the sycophant directly. The_s_is_silent couldn't be there in person, but she came up with the idea of wearing sheet masks. Diana would bring the towels she knew were in Devin's office. Then, using all the viral media footage of the disruption, they would call for a massive wave of user cancelations.

I had to make sure Maren never found out about the Slack channel.

I saw , I texted her. Holy shit.

Now what? Should I express my condolences, ask if there was anything I could do? I couldn't post anything publicly in defense of Devin or Richual or Evan, not until I found out what our official line was. I did what Devin would have done: to the internet, I pretended nothing was wrong.

"You okay?" Adam asked. "Can I get you a snack?"

"Stay there," I told him, and snapped a picture of him holding the screwdriver. **Work work work work work,** I wrote in the caption.

Could you do me a favor , Maren said, and ask Diana to go to the summit and get Devin's bag? It's in the green room it has her phone.

But Diana was no longer with us. She'd emailed her letter of resignation. I screenshotted it for Maren.

> Hey y'all,
>
> I will not have my labor further exploited by a company
> funded by a sexual predator and led by his sycophant. I
> acknowledge my privilege in that my parents have been
> paying my rent and living expenses during my internship so
> that if I quit, I will not be homeless. (Also, FYI my dad is a
> lawyer, just in case you were thinking of pressing charges for
> borrowing the towels. Think again!) For the sake of my future
> in the job market, I cannot have my personal brand
> associated with Richual. I want to give a shout-out to
> Khadijah, who has been a really great boss who literally
> supported my growth. Now I'm deleting my account. If you
> want to stay in touch, find me on Insta.

> Oh FFS. Can you ask Chloe?
> Chloe has Lyme disease.
> Right now?
> That's what she said. She's not here. I'll go.
> What would I do without you!!!!

In the Uber, I rolled down my window. The freezing air was like a caffeine injection, a buzz that gave me the illusion I could do this. "I think I should tell her that I'm pregnant now. Today. With you there," I told Adam. I had to deflect attention from what had happened at the conference and how much I knew about the behind-the-scenes plotting. If Maren was going to yell at me, I preferred she do it over my pregnancy rather than my negligence. Had she seen what was happening to our user numbers? I didn't want to know.

Adam smiled nervously. He was staring out the other window, tapping a rhythm on his thigh to a song I didn't recognize, possibly by Phish.

"You're freaking out," I said. "I need you to keep it together."

"I'm just worried about whether this level of stress is healthy for you and the baby."

"What are my options here?"

"What if you got a different job?"

I posed in my seat, one hand on my belly and the other behind my head like a mermaid. "Maternity model?"

I waited for Adam to say *he* would get a different job, but that wasn't the plan. Next month, we were getting an apartment together. After the baby came, he would be the primary caregiver, the Brooklyn dad in the BabyBjörn, and I would go back to work. I couldn't leave Richual. I had to stick it out for at least another three years, until my shares fully vested.

When Maren opened the door, she was barefoot, backlit by the sun flooding Devin's palatial open-plan apartment, which was more like a photography studio than a place where anyone actually lived. At her side, she held an open bottle of wine.

"Welcome," she said. "Welcome to ground zero. Please come in."

"This is my boyfriend, Adam."

"Nice to finally meet you," he said, reaching out a hand and then retracting it when he saw her beige wrist braces. "I came down last night to go to Khadijah's doctor appointment."

"Came down from where?"

"Dutchess County."

"How lovely that you have a home up there," Maren said, in a weird British accent. "It must be so nice to be able to escape the city, get away."

"It's not really my home. I'm actually helping a friend who—"

"Do you have the bag?" Maren whispered. "Devin's napping, but I'm going to hold her thumb up to the phone and unlock it. Do you think that will work?"

"Actually, there's something we wanted to tell you," Adam said, gripping my hand. *Thank you*, I thought, and squeezed back.

Maren looked at Adam's face, as if registering his features for the first time, and then at mine, putting them together.

"You're getting married! I'm so happy." She didn't look happy at all. "I have my license from the Universal Life Church if you need an officiant. It would be my honor. Let's put a pin in this and pick it up later. Cheers." She held the bottle out to us and then brought it to her lips, but it was empty.

"No," I said. She never listened. What made me think she would listen now? After all the mornings I came in early, all the nights I worked late, all the texts and emails I responded to on weekends because Adam was away so what else did I have to fill my time with but work, all the editorial content I put together for Cervical Health Awareness Month and National Endometriosis Awareness Month and Sexual Assault Awareness Month, all the staff photo shoots, where I sat front and center, smiling, the token black girl (everyone called each other babe: *Thanks, babe*; *no problem, babe*; *really sorry, babe*, but I was only ever Khadijah)— Maren used me when she needed me and I was supposed to be grateful for the opportunity. I wasn't negligent. I was over-worked.

I held Devin's purse hostage.

"Maren, I'm pregnant," I said. I stood up as tall as I could. "This is good news for you. It gives the company the chance to institute a progressive paid parental leave policy. It's good PR. It's also the perfect time to create a self-care content vertical specifi-cally for prenatal and postpartum millennials, which has so far been an untapped audience segment for us."

She held one hand to her forehead, massaging her temples. I couldn't tell if she was looking down at the floor or if she was looking for the bump underneath my coat, so I took it off. "My due date is in July. I'm asking for six weeks of maternity leave and another six weeks part-time after that."

"You're pregnant," she repeated.

"She's pregnant," Adam said.

"Khadijah, I'm surprised you think it's okay to just leave me like this."

I was seized by a cold chill.

"I'm not leaving," I said. "Not until July. And then I'll be back. Adam is going to be the primary caregiver. I believe in Richual. I believe in the work we're doing." *Stop talking*, I thought. *You're making it worse.*

"You're telling me this now? The day I learn that Devin is one of Evan's victims?" Her voice dropped to a hiss.

"To be fair," Adam said, looking at me, "she wanted to tell you sooner, but it never seemed like the right time."

"I would appreciate if you didn't mansplain to me in this situation."

"Wait," I said. "*Devin* is one of Evan's victims?"

"Yes and I think it's time for her to break her silence."

Before I could respond, Adam set Devin's bag down gently on the kitchen counter. "Great meeting you," he said, steering me out the door before Maren could suck me back into her vortex.

Devin

Arianna's lip is bleeding. I can see the blood on her front teeth. I should tell her. I should tell her that there is blood on her teeth. I don't want her to be embarrassed. I would want someone to tell *me*. Why didn't she moisturize her lips? I take one finger and put it in my own mouth, rub it along my top teeth, the way my mom used to, but Arianna isn't looking at me—she's giving a tinkly finger wave and scrunching her nose at someone she recognizes in the audience.

Then she grabs a phone from one of the masked women and starts recording a video. "It's so hard to say this," she says. "But I'm not going to hide it any longer. I won't be complicit. Devin was abused. Devin is a victim. I'm going to ask the Richual community to come together to support her during this difficult time."

When Arianna turns to look at me, her face has melted into my mom's face. Two streams of blood are running from her nostrils into her mouth.

"Evan touched me, too," she says to me. "He touched me when I was dead." She takes my hands and puts them on her breasts.

I woke up in bed in the dark, groggy from my nap, a sour taste in my mouth. "Maren?" I yelled.

The sound of her voice, speaking to someone in the living room. "Who's here?"

"Just me," she called back. The daylight was gone. I turned on the lamp on the nightstand, which was covered in dust and Starburst wrappers, a bottle of Kiehl's self-tanner that had leaked onto my copy of *The Clarity Cleanse*, and my Fitbit charger.

She brought me my phone in bed. "Khadijah picked it up. I didn't try to unlock your password or anything."

I had thirty-eight missed text messages, mostly from Katelyn. I scrolled for Evan's name. Nothing. Nothing. Nothing. Not even a You ok? No Call me if you need me. I'd defended him, hadn't I? I was sure he would text me later that night. He would offer to come over and this time we could talk. Really talk. I wanted to hear him say, *I'm worried about you.* It was my turn for sympathy. With my camera on selfie mode, I assessed the damage: my face was sleep-creased, my eyes bloodshot, my hair ratty and tangled, my eyeliner surprisingly intact. In low light, I looked like I'd just been fucked.

"Should I offer to bring you a sheet mask in bed?"

"Very funny," I said. I remembered why my mouth tasted like puke.

"Have you ever seen Evan's mask?"

"Evan's 'mask'?"

"It's something I found at his house."

"Don't tell me," I said. I didn't want to know what Maren knew that I didn't.

"On one side it says—"

"Don't *tell* me, I said."

"—'fuck' and on the other it says 'sleep.'"

Yes, I'd seen the mask. I had the same one in my nightstand. It was from Kiki de Montparnasse and cost $195. "So what?" I said, getting out of bed. My blouse was glued to my torso with sweat. At some point I'd taken off my pants.

"It just seems like he has a hard time distinguishing the difference between those two . . . states of being," Maren said.

"That's his thing," I said. "His Sleeping Beauty thing. I don't ask *you* about *your* sex life."

"I don't have a sex life. I have Zoloft."

I went to scrape my tongue in the bathroom and then drank a glass of room-temperature filtered water. If Evan would just text me, I could ask her to leave. I started tapping the energy meridian points on my face using the Emotional Freedom Technique. "Even though I have to appear perfect to survive," I whispered, "I deeply and completely accept myself. Even though I have to appear perfect to survive, I deeply—"

My phone rang. It was an unfamiliar number with a 212 area code.

"Hello? Evan?"

"Devin? Hey! It's Clem from Dragg and Dropp. I was at the summit this morning?" Her voice was rushed, breathless.

"Thank you so much for your concern, but I really can't talk right now."

"My crew got some incredible footage of your fireside chat that we can use for the pilot episode of *Stay Woke, Y'all*. In-cred-i-ble. It was such a visceral moment. I'm sure you felt that as well. We got a few interviews on-camera with Richual users who were at the event about the beach towel reveal and what it meant to them."

"What it meant to *them*?"

"What it means to live in a world where even women don't believe other women. This isn't even about Evan anymore, you have to understand that; it's about the culture. You don't know how to get in touch with Khadijah, do you? She hasn't responded to my last two emails. I need access to the Slack channel."

Maren was standing across from me at the kitchen island, mouthing, *Who is it?*

"No," I told Clementine. "I don't." And then I hung up.

My cofounder, my work wife, my business bestie was staring at me with total pity. Maren would always be stronger than me. It had something to do with where she came from, and what she'd overcome, growing up on the kind of food they sold at Walmart. She was solid as a punching bag. She wasn't desperately checking her phone for messages that said she mattered to someone, someone who would notice if she dropped dead. She could exist without validation. It was true what she said: I had a wine fridge, a monthly unlimited subscription to Pheel, an apartment that she would never be able to afford, not even to rent. So why was I so alone? Why didn't anyone want to share it with me?

"I quit," I told Maren. "You can have Richual. You can be CEO. I can't do it anymore."

"You can't quit," she sighed.

"Yes, I can. I'll go on a silent vipassana meditation retreat."

"And then what?"

"And then I'll . . . adopt a shelter dog." I knew I should just ask Maren to untangle the knot of *Stay Woke, Y'all* and get us out of it. But then I would have to admit how stupid I was for green-lighting a web series where women debated the stupidity of other women like me. The title was stupid, wasn't it? Had the title been my idea? Why hadn't Khadijah stopped me when she was in the room? Wasn't she supposed to be in charge of our content strategy?

"I just don't think I'm strong enough," I told Maren. "To be CEO."

"Bullshit," she said.

"You're a strong person, so you don't understand what it's like."

Maren leaned over the kitchen island until her face was nearly touching mine. Her teeth were ringed with purple stains. "That's why Evan chose you."

"Because I'm not strong?"

"No, because you *are*. This guy has a type. I'm sorry, but he does. He picks a powerful, successful woman, and then he assaults her while she's asleep. Do you have anything to eat that has cheese in it?" She was looking inside the fridge.

"Evan never assaulted me," I said.

I wanted to say, *How can it be assault if I like it?* I wanted to make Maren understand somehow what turned me on—to lie there in the dark, waiting, having nothing to do but pretend to be dreaming, taking pleasure from the absence of having to try so hard at anything. I had told Maren that Evan was my boyfriend as if this were the kind of fairy tale where saying the words out loud would make it so. But of course he wasn't my boyfriend. He was a drug without a reliable connection.

"Hot Pockets?"

They were left over from a binge.

"I'm not sure how old they are," I said, "but you can have them."

"Men have been oppressing women for centuries by keeping them from talking to each other. I just think you could help a lot of people. By being open."

"It's hard for me to talk about Evan and what we do together." *Don't cry*, I thought. *Do not cry*. "Because I feel like you're going to make me feel bad about myself."

Maren didn't say anything.

"I don't know if it's, like, 'feminist' or whatever, but I like that he has power over me. That's what makes it hot."

"I believe you."

"You do?"

"That's why they call it the cycle of abuse," Maren said. "That was in something I read online. It isn't all bad. Some of it feels really good. And then it gets bad again."

I thought of Evan's silence, the way he kept me on a leash waiting to hear from him. I remembered his hand under the table at the pitch meeting, finding a hole in my jeans, daring me to say anything. I felt unstable around him. But I still wanted him. Had he tricked me into wanting him? Was that abuse?

The microwave dinged. I stared at the twin Hot Pockets. The

yellow cheese oozed out the sides, spreading a greasy lake across the plate. Sauce bubbled through the crusty holes on top.

"That smells really good," I said.

"Have one."

"I can't. It'll make me sick."

"No, it won't," she said, handing me a fork.

I blew at the halo of steam and took a bite of the hot bland crust and runny cheese and felt the delicious hit of fat, the rush of humiliation.

Maren

Cheryl Strayed was always quoting this Rilke poem that read, "You must change your life," and that's what I was going to do.

I didn't drink all weekend. John made bacon and eggs on Saturday morning, and I held up my ten-dollar coconut water kale celery mango smoothie as evidence of my superiority and newfound devotion to treating my body like a temple. "Looks good on you, babe," he said, after we had a conversation about how important it is to have a positive mindset. He was reading a book on how to make more money using the law of attraction, and I was reading posts on Richual about how the more closely I followed a plant-based diet, the more I would only crave foods from a plant-based diet. The way celery tasted, it had to be good for you.

At a clothing boutique with an ampersand in the title, I bought one pink dress in a size 14 and another identical dress in a size 12 that I could manifest my body into later. The pink dress had a silk necktie collar that was at once understated and frustrat-ingly complicated to knot—I thought Devin would appreciate it.

After I recorded the video about how I believed women should support other women and that's why I could no longer be com-plicit in hiding the fact that Devin was a victim of Evan's abuse, the messages of support flooded in. I posted the video to Devin's own account and there were more than a thousand comments al-ready, from the influencers modeling athleisure wear made from recycled iPhone cases who saw Devin as their guru, but also from the endlessly outraged, woke contingent of our users, the femi-nists who were usually first to pounce on Devin for not sufficiently apologizing for her privilege in every single one of her posts. Her victimhood united our user base. I had cracked the code on what brought all women together. With her phone in hand, I also changed the tagline in Devin's Richual profile from "Total Boss and Self-Care Addict" to "Total Boss, Survivor."

We love you, Devin. Stay strong. #BelieveVictims. She was for-given for her beach towel sin. Even Rachelle Tanaka created a Richual account so she could post a selfie captioned, **I forgive you, Devin**. Then she posted again twenty minutes later with a coupon code for a VR fitness software pack. @PaleOhHellNo put together a video montage of different Richual users talking about how hard it is to talk about things that are so hard to talk about and gave me a shout-out for modeling what was possible for the loved ones of survivors. @GypseaLee turned the nine-second footage of Devin's face at the summit into a PSA about how long it can take for a woman to realize that she is a victim.

I'd given Devin what she always wanted: sympathy and attention. We had more user activity in forty-eight hours than we'd had since the election. I knew I could leverage this.

I drank four liters of water and redeemed my twenty-eight-day reboot program from Euphebe that Devin got me for Christmas so I could "lose weight and feel fabulous by resetting" my health "without hunger and deprivation." In the app store, I found a visualization meditation for detoxifying the liver. John was redecorating his home office (a closet with a chair and a desk that folded down from the wall on a hinge) with newspaper clippings and mantras: "Wealth Matters" and "Money Is Energy." I told him if he got his novel down to five hundred pages, I would read it.

By Sunday night, I was feeling extremely hydrated and brave. Here if you want to talk, I texted Devin.

I cleaned our entire bathroom, throwing away old bottles of Avon liquid foundation and autumnal-scented candles, scrubbing the grout between the tiles with unprecedented vigor and attention to detail, and then I took selfies in the freshly Windexed mirror, wearing my BreastNest and a pair of black underwear.

Ghost white stretch marks laid tracks down my outer thighs. My left boob drooped lower than my right. The cellulite on the underside of my upper arms was something I tried not to think about. I had no illusions that my body would transform overnight, or that I would ever be able to wear a crop top in public, but I didn't see how I was going to change my life if I couldn't confront reality. I was aging. I was almost thirty-two. Before posting, I zoomed in to be sure none of my pubic hair was showing in the selfie.

This is the first "before" pic I've ever posted, I wrote in the caption.

> In a way, it's also an "after." I've been working to build Richual for about two years now and somewhere along the way I stopped taking care of myself. My work wife, my best friend @DevinAvery has helped me see how much farther I still have to go on my self-care journey. Two years ago, I don't think I ever would have even written the phrase "self-care journey" lol. That's how much Richual has changed my life.
>
> I have a confession to make. I have a drinking problem. That's the scariest thing I've ever said in public. I tried to hide my problem from my coworkers, my partner, my family. This week, I finally realized that I was more afraid that I would never be able to stop than I was of asking for help. If this post helps one person feel seen with whatever she's struggling with, then my reluctant visibility will have been worth it.

I tapped my messages icon to see if Devin had responded. Nothing.

The post had one like, two likes, three likes, four. I thumbed refresh. I waited. More.

...

The board meeting was scheduled for Monday morning. To be discussed: hitting the benchmarks that would solidly position us

as the Instagram of wellness and finalizing our strategy and timeline for raising $25 million.

I arrived early, dressed up like a woman in my new pink dress
and a lipstick I found when I was cleaning out the bathroom called
GoGetter. In the staff kitchen, I cut fresh cucumbers and put them
in the water pitcher the way Devin liked. I borrowed a few potted
succulents from Khadijah's desk to make a centerpiece on the conference table. On one wall of the conference room, an artist had
stenciled a Kanye tweet. On another, we had a quote from Roxane
Gay: "I embrace the label of bad feminist because I am human."

Our investors Klaus Wu and Richard Zimmerman would video-
conference in from Menlo Park. I had one chance to make my case
for why we should abandon our series B plan altogether and pivot to
a paid membership structure—let our users themselves pay for the
value we were providing, instead of being so reliant on corporate
advertising. What could be more positive for women than women
paying to use a product built and owned by other women?

It would give us more freedom in the kind of content we could
put out there—if we wanted to call out a beauty brand for doing
animal testing, we could, without worrying about that brand canceling their ad spend. I had proof of how high our user engagement
was. All we had to do was roll out the new membership model
quickly. Plus, raising more capital would mean adding more seats
to our board, and I didn't think we needed any more men at the
table. Devin and I were already outnumbered three to two.

With the matches we kept in the kitchen for birthdays, I lit a
bundle of sage and cleared the space of toxic energy.

Khadijah arrived at 9:55. I had asked if she would take the minutes while I was busy presenting.

"I stopped drinking," I blurted out. "I'm really sorry that you had to see me like that."

"Yeah, I saw your post," she said.

She was more dressed up than usual, in a white blazer over a black maternity dress. Her baby bump seemed so obvious, I was mortified I hadn't noticed it sooner.

"You look nice today," she added.

I'll organize a baby shower at the office, I thought. I'd have it catered. All the money I used to spend on wine could now go to generosity toward others. I would make it up to her. I could enlist the help of Khadijah's closest friends at work to help with the decorations. I tried to think of who those friends might be. I could call Adam. At least I remembered his name.

In the Google Doc with our meeting agenda, I added a section on *Content strategy for prenatal and postpartum millennials*.

Anonymous badger was editing the doc at the same time.

Staff, they wrote. I had no idea who the badger was. Could have been Devin, could have been Evan, could have been Klaus.

Under *Staff*, I added a bullet point: *Let's talk about benefits esp. paid parental leave.*

I poured Khadijah a glass of cucumber water.

Devin and Evan entered the room together and sat next to each other in silence, leaving one empty chair between them like something left unspoken. Devin's face was pale and somber. She wouldn't make eye contact with me. She was wearing a black poncho that went past her knees, her hair braided around her crown like a Scandinavian child's.

Of course she was in a bad mood—she thought we had to continue riding the fundraising merry-go-round as if nothing had changed. Neither Klaus nor Richard reached out to me about the allegations against Evan, which meant the story didn't even cross their desks, or they didn't see an issue with Evan's conduct. They didn't have their own Richual accounts, so it was unlikely they saw my video either.

I hoped Devin would be able to hear the subtext of my pitch. If we switched to a paid membership model, we didn't have to raise more money from Klaus or Richard or any other VC. We didn't need Evan to open doors for us. We would be women-funded, free from men altogether.

"Hello," said the head of Klaus on the big TV screen. He was wearing a blue plaid shirt, unbuttoned, under a blazer.

"Hello, it's Richard," said Richard. He was wearing a green plaid shirt, unbuttoned, no blazer.

"Hello, Richard? It's Klaus, but your video isn't coming through."

"We can see both of you," I said.

"Should I restart my browser?" asked Richard.

"Ah, there you are," said Klaus.

"Good morning, everyone," I said. "Thank you for joining us so early on the West Coast."

"We're just waiting on one more," Evan said.

"Who?" I asked.

"Can we hold off for five?" Evan asked. He had to be high if he thought I was going to let him run this meeting.

"No, I don't want waste anyone's time. Khadijah, would you please do the roll call?"

"Devin Avery, present. Maren Gelb, present. Evan Wiley—"

Our lawyer, Leslie Royce, walked in. We weren't yet big enough to have in-house counsel, but Leslie was someone we called on when we needed her to review a contract or help us untangle a sticky situation with an advertising partner. She was old enough to be the mom of anyone in the room, but she had no children. Devin had known her for years; Leslie had worked with her dad.

"I wasn't aware that you were joining us," I said.

"Sorry about that miscommunication, Maren," she said, shaking my hand before taking the seat between Devin and Evan. "We're all good."

"Are we? All good?"

"For the record," Evan said, "Maren, I think you've done a great job."

Khadijah looked to me, as if seeking permission to enter this into her notes, and I nodded.

"Thank you, Evan, I'll take it from here. I know that funding strategy is on the top of our agenda, and I have a creative solution that I'm excited to share with everyone. First, let me just bring up this screen so you can see our live user metrics. It's Monday morning, so there isn't a whole lot happening right now, but if you look at this huge peak here, that represents the spike we experienced this weekend."

"How do you explain the spike?" asked Klaus.

"We're really seeing an uptick in women sharing vulnerable stories they may not feel comfortable posting to other platforms, like Facebook or Twitter. I think that's part of our value prop, the safe space element, and I see a way to turn it into a revenue-generating opportunity."

I brought up a slide with my projections.

"This is a forecast of what's possible if we pivot to a paid-subscription model. If we have two million active users paying $1.99 a month, or $19.99 a year, that's between forty and fifty million dollars in annual revenue. That's ten times what we make in advertising."

Richard was laughing. "There's just one problem."

"I'm definitely open to feedback," I said.

"Social media is free for the user. It's an advertising-supported model. You collect data, you sell it to advertisers, the value is passed on to the user. I know you're a smart woman, Maren. I'm not telling you anything you don't know."

"He's saying that people don't want to pay for something they've already been getting for free," Devin explained. "No one likes to feel tricked." It was the first thing she'd said to me all morning. She hadn't even complimented my dress.

I inhaled a deep breath through the open and nonthreatening smile I'd plastered to my face. "How will we know it's a bad idea unless we try? Klaus, thoughts?"

"I agree with Richard."

I didn't give Evan an opportunity to contribute.

"We're offering a product for women, by women. Women want to support other women. We saw that this weekend. When women stand together, there's power. Let's harness that power. Everybody wins. Khadijah also has a great idea about creating more content that speaks to an untapped demographic, but I don't want to speak for her, so I'll let her fill you in."

Khadijah started to say something and then stopped herself. They were all looking at me, the men in boxes on the TV screen, Leslie with her red reading glasses and her long black hair cut by a streak of white, Evan's calm and inscrutable mug, Devin testy and unfocused.

"I guess that's my cue?" Leslie asked.

"Maren Gelb," she continued, reading aloud from a document, "based upon an internal review conducted at the behest of the board of directors, we have found your behavior to be manipulative and disruptive, as you broke into the CEO's password-protected, personal Richual account to post a slanderous video that distorts a consensual sexual relationship between two adults. By your own admission here today, you did so in order to dishonestly inflate user traffic on the platform. The board is also concerned about your alcohol use and how it reflects on the company brand."

I sat perfectly still as I began to lose track of my body in space. I would not move my head. I stared at the table. The $2,600 reclaimed wood conference table. They set me up. No one told me. They didn't let me prepare.

"Leslie, I'll be the first to admit that I have developed a drinking problem, mostly due to the pressures and pace of trying to make this company the unicorn I know it can be." I tried to remember which camera to look into so that Klaus and Richard would catch my meaningful eye contact. "But I assure you—I assure the board—that I'm addressing it. I stopped drinking two days ago. I'll go to treatment if you want me to. I'll go to AA. But I did not take advantage of a single person in this room or at this company. If anyone took advantage, it's Evan. Why isn't he under internal review?"

She continued reading. "Based on our findings, your employment is hereby terminated immediately. The good news is that we have put together a generous offer to buy your shares of Richual."

Leslie put a copy of the document in front of me, along with a check for $187,500. It was the largest amount of money I had ever seen in my life. It was also missing a zero.

I waved the check at Devin. "Is this missing a zero?"

Her mouth was trembling, but her jaw was set.

"Devin? Hello? What is this bullshit? Now you can't talk to me? After everything we've been through? You had to go behind my back like a tattletale? What is this, fifth grade? I want you to say it to my face. Say that I 'manipulated' you."

She began to cry silently.

"You're such a victim. It's amazing. I'm the bully. I get it. I'm the bad guy." I had never hit another person, but I understood now what that surge of electricity felt like, the need to make rage manifest.

"Maren, I'm really sorry, but you're out of control."

I slept in your bed when your dad died, you ungrateful cunt, I thought. I turned back to Leslie.

"How is it ethical that you're our lawyer, but you're also Devin's lawyer?"

"I'm not here to represent Devin. I'm here to represent the best interests of Richual."

"You all threw me under the bus. All of you." I looked at Khadijah. "I have the right to my own representation. And how is twenty percent of a five-million-dollar valuation only one hundred eighty-seven thousand five hundred dollars?"

"You may want to refresh your memory of the vesting schedule you agreed to when you signed the founders agreement."

"Okay, fine, then I keep the shares until they fully vest. You can terminate me, but I still own twenty percent of the company."

Leslie sighed. "Technically, we don't have to buy your shares at all. We could terminate you *and* keep them, because of the seriousness of your transgressions. I hope you'll consider our offer. And of course you have the right to your own representation."

Klaus and Richard blinked onscreen, unmoved. Another startup with founder drama, so what? I was cheap, disposable. They knew I couldn't afford to turn down the buyout offer. I waited in vain for someone to tell me I was irreplaceable. The whole platform would collapse without me. No one knew how to do what I did.

"So I guess you're searching for a new COO then?" I asked. "Good luck with that."

"Actually, we have one," Evan said. "The youngest black pregnant millennial ever promoted to the C-suite. Katelyn's working on the press release now."

I looked at Khadijah. She held my gaze.

...

I was walking down Fifth Avenue in the cold, without direction, dumb with shock, unable to imagine how to tell John my life had just been changed without my consent, scanning the block for the best place where I could reasonably be left alone to consume a carafe of mimosas, when I recognized the banner.

"You Must Change Your Life," it said, on a cotton T-shirt that cost forty-nine dollars. I took it as a sign. I bought gold-flecked compression tights and a zip-front, movement-reducing, high-octane performance sports bra. I was a hundred-thousandaire now; the world was my oyster. A woman named Elecktra helpfully entered my credit card information for a recurring monthly unlimited pass, the first month discounted for Pheel virgins.

It was still bright day, but the velvet curtains were drawn and a row of white pillar candles threw flickering shadows on the walls. For the darkness I was grateful. The studio was as warm as a womb. I tried to fold my legs underneath myself in a way that projected both my fragility and strength. There was a surprising number of women putting their mats down in alignment with little purple hearts at 11:15 in the morning. *Get a job*, I thought. I almost reached for my phone to check my email before I remembered I didn't have a job. Stevie Nicks sang softly in the background.

"Welcome to your container," a woman with the body of an orchid stem said.

"Thank you," I said.

"Any recent injuries I should know about?" She put one hand on my shoulder and I almost started crying.

I didn't know what to say. I didn't know how to tell her I wanted out of this body and into another. The only word I could think of to describe my wound was *women*.

"No injuries," I said. "But I haven't worked out in a while."

"If it gets to be too much, just go into child pose.

"For those of you who don't know me, I'm Tressa," she continued, speaking into her headset now. "I once had surgery. They told me I would have to relearn how to walk. They told me there would be pain. They said, here, take a pill for your pain. And I said—" Tressa turned up the volume on Kings of Leon and then turned herself upside down, against the wall.

I knew this was going to hurt. I knew my arms would tire and my legs would give out. At some point I'd be lying on the floor, unable to catch my breath, watching stars behind my eyes, regretting every decision that brought me here. But I also knew the music was going to get louder and louder until it sheltered us, a room full of women willing to do anything to our bodies if it drowned out the sound of our minds, each of us screaming for our own reasons, in the dark.

Acknowledgments

Thank you to all the women who supported me while I worked on this book: Kat Rosenfield, Julia Strayer, Alizah Salario, Julia Phillips, Jennie Baird, Sandra Rodriguez Barron, Laura Feinstein, Grace Do, Claire Dunnington, Elizabeth Trundle, Ingrid Aybar, Maggie Levine, Sarah Vogel, Sharon Shula, Lynne Greene, Roseline Glazer, and Raz Tal.

Erin Hosier and Margaux Weisman, you sprinkle the spirit dust on top of everything. I could not have written this without your encouragement, sage advice, and regular dosage of relevant links. You are my favorite influencers.

I am so lucky that *Self Care* has a home at Penguin Books. Patrick Nolan, Lindsay Prevette, Mary Stone, Allison Carney, Sara Delozier, Bel Banta, Lynn Buckley, Jennifer Eck, and Alicia Cooper: thank you for all your creative ideas, your enthusiasm, and your exceptional attention to detail.

I am grateful to the Ragdale Foundation for the gift of time and space to develop my work.

Brian Jacks deserves all the credit for making me laugh and keeping me sane.

Land of Enchantment

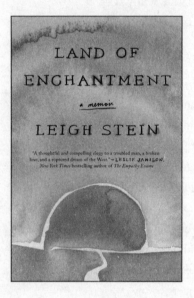

With searing honesty and cutting humor, Leigh Stein explores the heartbreaking complexity of why the person hurting you the most can be impossible to leave. Set against the stark and surreal landscape of New Mexico, *Land of Enchantment* is a coming-of-age memoir about young love, obsession, and loss, and how a person can imprint a place in your mind forever.

"A thoughtful and compelling elegy to a troubled man, a broken love, and a broken dream of the west." –Leslie Jamison, *New York Times* best-selling author of *The Empathy Exams*

 PLUME

 PENGUIN BOOKS